I0712466

Just One Shot

 THE BILLIONAIRE BARONS OF TEXAS — BOOK SIX

CHRIS KENISTON

Indie House Publishing

Indie House Publishing

MORE BOOKS
By Chris Keniston

The Billionaire Barons of Texas
Just One Date
Just One Spark
Just One Dance
Just One Take
Just One Taste
Just One Shot
Just One Chance

Hart Land
Heather
Lily
Violet
Iris
Hyacinth
Rose
Calytrix
Zinnia
Poppy
Picture Perfect

Farraday Country
Adam
Brooks
Connor
Declan
Ethan
Finn
Grace
Hannah
Ian
Jamison

Keeping Eileen
Loving Chloe
Morgan
Neil
Owen

Honeymoon Series
Honeymoon for One
Honeymoon for Three
Honeymoon for Four
Honeymoon for Five
Honeymoon for Six

Aloha Romance Series:
Aloha Texas
Almost Paradise
Mai Tai Marriage
Dive Into You
Look of Love
Love by Design
Love Walks In
Shell Game
Flirting with Paradise

Surf's Up Flirts:
(Aloha Series Companions)
Shall We Dance
Love on Tap
Head Over Heels
Perfect Match
Just One Kiss
It Had to Be You
Cat's Meow

CHAPTER ONE

"Is it always this hot in Texas?" Siobhan's friend and former college roommate, Bridget, waved her hand in front of her face. As if that was actually going to help.

Her gaze fixed ahead, Siobhan didn't bother to look up. "You've heard the expression, fry an egg on the sidewalk?"

Squinting at the sunlight, Bridget nodded.

"Texas invented it."

"I think next time I visit, I'll pick a cooler month."

Her camera centered on a baby bird pecking at the dirt under a scraggly shrub, Siobhan snapped the shot before facing her friend. "Probably October. As long as rain doesn't bother you."

"I think I'd rather be soggy than melting."

Siobhan chuckled. Her friend did have a point.

"Remind me again, why we're traipsing out here in this horrid heat?"

"State Fair." Texas has some of the most undervalued national parks in the country. If she wanted her photographic career to flourish at a level suitable to the Baron name, she needed some recognition. A friend of her sister's who owned an art gallery suggested that winning a ribbon or two at the Texas State Fair would fit the bill. Animal and nature photos dominated the history of award-winning photography, and the Texas parks had both in abundance.

Bridget unscrewed the cap on her warm water bottle and guzzled what was left inside. "You've got twenty, thirty minutes tops to get your prize photograph and then we're heading back to the hotel for a water refill." Bridget's mouth tipped up in the closest thing to a smile Siobhan had seen all day. "And a dip in the pool to cool off sounds pretty good too."

Once again, her friend had a good point. The heat was a *tad* oppressive this time of year. "Deal."

Now a true grin spread across Bridget's face.

Ten minutes later, Siobhan lowered her gaze along the precipice to one side and spotted the perfect shot. "There."

Bridget's gaze danced left and right, then up and around. "There where?"

Leaning against a boulder, her arm outstretched, Siobhan pointed at the lone pink bloom thriving amongst the rocky side. "Right there. That flower."

When Bridget's gaze reached the end of Siobhan's finger and settled on the flower, a deep frown formed between her brows. "Doesn't look like much of a shot to me."

"Oh, it will be." In her mind, Siobhan could see it now. She just had to get, "Closer."

"What?" Bridget inched forward, glanced at the drop only a few feet away, and eased back. "There has to be another… hey, be careful."

Standing at the very edge of the hillside, Siobhan tipped her head and her camera but there was no way she could get the angle she wanted. Blowing out a deep breath, she looked up. Even she didn't have the nerve to climb along the rocky edge to get closer. Maybe if she had the right equipment, but not barehanded. And then she spotted it. A lone tree up above.

"I don't like that look." Her hand shading her eyes, Bridget lifted her gaze upward. "Whatever you're thinking, this is a bad…hey. Where are you going?"

Anxious to get her shot while the sunlight was behind her, Siobhan took off up the narrow path at a fast clip. "The tree."

"Tree?" Bridget followed, her attention on the rocky path. "Are you sure you Barons aren't part mountain goat? Slow down."

"I don't have much time."

"You have your whole life ahead of you. That is unless we fall off this cliff. Slow down."

"There." The lone tree stood strong and tall, if a little lifeless.

"What do you want with a dead tree?" Bridget inched left, avoiding the edge of the rocky path. There was no missing the moment her gaze shifted from the drop to her right, then back to Siobhan. A gasp could have been heard clear across the ravine. "Get off that tree!"

Already halfway up the trunk, Siobhan was convinced the roots were firmly planted and even if there was little life left in the tree, all she needed was to reach that first limb and she'd be able to shimmy across for her shot.

"Siobhan Pegeen Baron, get down here right this minute!" Stomping her foot hard on the ground, Bridget dropped her fisted hands on her hips. "You're going to get yourself killed for a stupid photograph."

"It's not stupid, and I'm not going to…Oops!" Her foot skidded away from the rough bark and feeling the tug of gravity against her well-rounded Irish derriere, Siobhan quickly hugged the tree with both arms.

"Oh, dear lord. Your mother will never forgive me. You scoot back here right this minute!"

Siobhan didn't have to look down at her friend to know the woman was both spitting mad and terrified. Now that Siobhan was literally out on a limb, there was no point in turning back without the shot. Releasing one arm to move the camera still dangling from her neck, Siobhan shifted her weight more heavily onto the massive branch.

"You're not listening to me."

"Just another minute." Unable to balance both her weight and the camera, Siobhan set her favorite camera on the branch and with a little scooting forward, clicked away. A cloud rolled by, creating partial shade beside the flower and she clicked some more. Mother Nature was wonderful.

The photograph taken, convinced the blue ribbon would be hers with these shots, she just had one thing to figure out. How the heck was she going to get out of this tree without getting herself killed?

All Jack Preston needed was a few hours of shut eye and he'd be able to do more than sleep in his soup tonight. Loosening his bow tie, he shoved it in his pocket and undid the shirt button that had been choking him for hours. When he'd donned this penguin suit last night, he'd expected to be home, or at least in bed, long before sunrise. What he hadn't expected was an after-party to end all after-parties.

The last two hours felt like he'd been swept back in time to a mid-century musical blockbuster. Seriously, not till last night had he ever seen an entire room of guests singing around a grand piano for hours except for in old movies. Dancing with every able-bodied single female in attendance was nothing unusual, but doing so until the sun sparkled through the penthouse windows and Devlin Baron's maid served the surviving twenty or thirty guests breakfast was another first.

Somehow between chatting up a stacked blonde he'd hoped to set a few sparks off with, being roped into reliving his and Devlin's senior year performances in *Godspell*, and the most ridiculous game of charades that had everyone laughing till they cried, Connie Danner had caught him in a moment of weakness and sweet-talked him into being her last-minute plus-one to a black-tie wedding. Another blasted wedding. Tonight. This last year he'd been to more weddings than he had in the previous decade. When Andrew Baron married, the core group of college buddies who thought nothing of zipping over to Monaco for a good yacht party on a moment's notice hadn't been seriously affected. By the time his best party buddy, Kyle, married and hung up his party hat, a domino effect of falling bachelors seemed to have started. The newest crop of most eligible bachelors weren't the same as his long-time cohorts.

Less than ten minutes on the road and his phone sounded, his mother's name flashing on his dashboard. With a tap of his steering wheel, he picked up the call.

"Hey, Mom."

"You're late."

Glancing quickly at the clock in front of him, he frowned, forcing his mind to run through late for what.

"Margaret is muttering in the kitchen. You know how she hates keeping food warm."

Brunch. "Sorry, Mom. I'll be there in about fifteen minutes."

"See you then, Son." The softness returned to her voice. "Love you."

"Love you too." No matter how tired he might be, his mom's routine of saying love you rather than goodbye, always made him smile.

At the next stop light, he rolled up his sleeves, undid another button on his shirt, and made a mental note to grab his loafers from the trunk and ditch the dress shoes. Even though he was no longer a teen needing to sneak around from his parents' oversight, he could at least try and not make it too obvious that he'd been out all night.

His phone dinged with a message as he pulled onto his family's property. The dashboard spat out that Connie needed to be at the church an hour early to dress with the girls, but her car was making funny noises on the drive home and would he please pick her up instead of meeting her there. Though he'd rather have had a few extra minutes to nap this afternoon, it looked like he was going to be hanging out at an empty church waiting for another wedding. Parked in front of the house, he tapped out *No Problem* and slipping the phone into his pocket, darted up the front steps.

Already seated at the table, his father casually let his gaze scan Jack from head to toe and back before familiar deep-set lines formed between his brows. "Late night?"

Jack resisted the urge to make excuses and simply dipped his chin before leaning over his mother's side for a quick hug and kiss hello. "Still playing bridge this afternoon?"

Smiling sweetly, his mother spread jam on a croissant and nodded. "The McKenzies are in Europe so we're playing with the Whitehalls. Should be interesting."

Serving himself from the buffet sideboard, he pulled up an image of the Whitehalls in his mind. "Isn't she the one who cheats at cards?"

"They both do," his father muttered over the coffee cup at his lips.

"We have a plan." His mother's grin turned sly. "We're going to insist the men play against the women. Tiffany won't have a partner to signal."

Jack smiled at his mother. The woman always had a solution for any problem.

"Speaking of partners." His father set his coffee cup down on the table. "You're not getting any younger."

And here came the familiar song and dance. Ever since Jack's thirty-fifth birthday, his father had been more insistent that it was time for him to settle down. Ever since Kyle's wedding, his father had found a way to work the subject into every and any conversation. "None of us are."

"You know what I mean." His father reached for a warm croissant and split it open. "Even Kyle Baron smartened up and found a nice wife. At this rate you're going to be wearing dentures and raising kids at the same time."

"No need to exaggerate, Dad. I'm not that old."

"You're not that young either."

Touché. It wasn't like Jack didn't envy Kyle and his brothers just a little bit, but some men weren't cut out for settling down. Jack didn't have it in him to be domesticated. His father would simply have to accept sooner or later that watching TV with the little woman and changing diapers was not in the cards for Jack.

CHAPTER TWO

"**D**on't look back until I tell you." Adjusting the light meter on her camera, Siobhan glanced in the direction of the impatient groom.

Normally, Siobhan would be the assistant and backup photographer for her friend Marilyn's wedding photography biz, but when Marilyn tripped down a flight of stairs two days ago unpleasantly snapping her ankle, Siobhan was promoted to main photographer for today's wedding of Mindy and Chad. Not wanting to disappoint Marilyn, or the bride, Siobhan needed to get the shot perfect. This was the photo that every bride loved. Capturing the groom's reaction when he first saw her in her wedding dress.

The brick arches under the canopy of massive trees outside the church was the best setting for bridal photos she'd ever seen. So far all the solo photos of the bride were going to be amazing. Especially the ones by some exotic plant that had the bride squealing when she'd seen it the first time. Now it was up to Siobhan to capture the arched background, the exotic plant, and the groom in a single shot.

"How much longer?" Chad stretched his neck, knowing better than to mess with the perfect bow tie that had taken the wedding coordinator longer than it should have to set straight. "It's hot out here in this monkey suit."

"Another moment, I promise." She had to bite back the urge to remind him the only options in a Texas summer were hot, hotter, and hottest.

Since the last-minute assistant that was supposed to be helping Siobhan was a no-show, setting up the shots and moving the equipment around was taking longer than she wanted. At least the bride stood waiting in the air-conditioned vestibule with the bridesmaids. No need to risk melting the woman of the day or ruining the perfect hair and makeup that had taken hours to get right. Using the elbow of her long sleeve black shirt, Siobhan wiped at her brow, longing for an Irish summer instead of this Texas oven. With a wave of her arm, she silently signaled the maid of honor to bring out the bride.

This whole process would have been so much easier had she not been doing the work of two people. She couldn't mess up this photo, she was sure it would be the cornerstone of the couple's wedding album. Or wedding website since no one printed albums anymore. Everything was stored on the cloud now.

Stepping away from the camera, she'd carefully set up, she hurried to where the bride stood.

"Where do you want me?" Mindy asked softly.

"Right here." Carefully glancing up at the sun and turning the bride to the right angle, Siobhan took an extra minute to make sure the hair, veil, and flowers were literally picture perfect.

"Is it time to look?" the groom called out without turning his head.

"No!" Siobhan and the bride shouted in unison before giggling at the unexpected synchronization.

"He's anxious to see you. That's a good sign." Siobhan winked at the woman. No need to relay that the man simply wanted out of the heat.

A last second check of the camera to record the video of their first look at each other, and the camera for the still photos, she studied the screens of both. It was time.

She clicked on the video. "Turn around, Chad."

With her other camera in hand, she clicked away as she captured the magic of the groom seeing his bride in her dress for the first time. Chad's eyes turned misty and his nervous stance relaxed.

"Well?" Mindy's smile was stiff and her voice quiet. Poor thing was so nervous.

"You are the most beautiful woman on this earth." Chad's voice cracked ever so slightly.

The bride's smile bloomed, the groom brushed his thumb across her cheek and whispered something only Mindy could hear. The sparkle in the couple's eyes was everything a photographer could ask for. The moment captured on film was as priceless as Siobhan had hoped it to be. Marilyn would be proud of her.

Since it would be dark when the ceremony was over, the couple had opted for doing their formal photos now beforehand.

Chad took Mindy's hands. "I'm so happy to be marrying you today."

"I love you," the bride whispered back, leaning in for a kiss.

"None of that now." Siobhan waved a hand at the couple. "We have photos to take before the guests inside revolt." She'd put in a last-minute text to her sisters for some help, but everyone in the family was tied up. So far, so good. At least the bridesmaids were trying to help when they weren't laughing and joking about.

The first batch of photos went off without a hitch. Everyone cooperated and the blissful couple managed to keep their hands to themselves. Now came the new effort, moving the entire entourage to the church steps. Just a few photos and the main show could begin.

Siobhan turned off her equipment. Two of the bridesmaids helped to carry the bride's train as she walked up to the church steps. Siobhan shrugged one camera onto her shoulder, but she couldn't get a good grip of the second one. There was no time to make two trips; they were dangerously close to behind schedule. So much so that she actually considered pulling a stranger off the street to help. She didn't even want to think how she was going to pull off the next few hours. "One shot at a time," she muttered, and reached for the equipment bag again, still muttering, "one shot at a time."

★

At the back of the air-conditioned church, Jack sat scrolling through his phone. The pew wasn't what anyone would consider comfortable, but there wasn't anything else to do until his date was done with photos.

Connie poked her head into the church from the vestibule. "You doing okay?"

He waved a hand. "I'm great."

"These photos are going to be spectacular. Mindy looks fabulous and the photographer seems really sharp. You could come out and watch. Stretch your legs."

"Sure." He slipped his phone into his breast pocket. For the most part, every bride always looked beautiful on her wedding day. It was no surprise that Connie's friend looked fabulous. For those in love and happy to marry, more power to them. None of that was in the cards for him. Like babies are all cute, brides are all beautiful. The problem is the lifelong commitment that goes with both children and wives. He wished the groom all the happiness in the world, but he liked being free to travel, party, or enjoy a woman's company no strings attached. Even if some of his friends were getting married lately and seemed more than a little happy, for him, marriage—to his parents' chagrin—was a hard pass.

Jack rose and a well-dressed older woman in the pew in front of him turned, her smile did little to hide her curiosity as to why he was leaving. He smiled back and followed Connie out of the church. The heat hit him hard. Born and raised in Texas, he was more than used to the summer heat, but that didn't mean he had to like it. For a split second, he'd reconsidered leaving the air-conditioned church.

The bridesmaids were lined up on the steps, shuffling back and forth according to height. Not far from the foot of the steps, the photographer juggled miscellaneous bags and equipment, reminding him of an overloaded pack mule. He didn't want to be in the way, but she looked like she needed help, and his mother would have his head for not helping a damsel in distress. "I'm going to give the photographer a hand."

Connie shrugged. "She's doing okay so far."

Turning back to the petite woman, she didn't look like she was doing okay to him. No sooner did she hike one of the cameras further onto her shoulder, then one or both would slip off as she reached for another load of equipment. "I don't know about that."

"Siobhan's a professional, but it's up to you."

An uncommon name in Texas, he squinted as he walked toward the woman. Could it be? No. There had to be more women named Siobhan than his best friend's little sister. Closing in, the cherub face looked up at him and he blinked. Good grief.

How long since he'd seen her? Since Kyle had settled down, he frankly didn't see as much of any of the Barons as he used to. On top of that, Siobhan spent most of her time in Ireland with her mom. Doing some fast math, the last time he remembered seeing her had to be three, maybe four years ago at Andrew's wedding. From across the lawn, the woman in black he knew to be the wedding coordinator was trotting across the lawn. Apparently, he wasn't the only one to notice the damsel in distress. The two reached Siobhan at almost the same instant. He raised his hand and smiled at the coordinator, who looked more nervous than the bride. "I've got this."

Once again, as the petite woman looked up from reaching for the tripod, one camera slid off her shoulder and almost touched the ground before she reached over to snatch it, knocking the other strap off of her shoulder till it settled on her elbow.

"Jack?" She straightened to her full height. "What are you doing here?"

He wished her startled tone didn't lean toward annoyed.

"I'm a plus-one." He pointed to where Connie stood on the lower steps watching them before leaning over to grab as much equipment as he could balance. "You should really have help."

"Tell me something I don't know." She hefted the one remaining bag onto her shoulder. "My help is a no-show."

Jack glanced at his date still intently watching his every move before tossing a smile in Siobhan's direction. "Then it looks like I'm all yours."

Her brows shot up and her eyes rounded into perfect circles.

The double entendre smacked him between the eyes. *Nice going, big brother's best friend. Go ahead and scare the crud out of the kid.* Time to backpedal and get his size twelve foot out of his mouth. "Consider me your photography assistant for the evening."

A smile replaced the startled expression and relief washed over him. At least he didn't have to worry now about one or all of her big brothers slowly tearing him apart limb from limb for making an untoward comment to their baby sister.

"Normally I would say absolutely not. But at least for the next bit, any help is appreciated. Just do as I say."

"Yes, ma'am." If he'd had a free hand he would have saluted.

The next few minutes went by in a flash. In a matter of seconds, Siobhan rearranged the bridesmaids order in what was clearly a more pleasing presentation than the one the girls had come up with on their own. Next were the groomsmen and the groom. Then photos of the maid of honor and bride, best man and groom, then the four of them. It didn't take long for Jack to realize the girl had an eye for this. What he couldn't remember was had her brothers ever mentioned she was a wedding photographer? Heck, had they even mentioned she'd graduated high school? No, he knew that, last he'd heard, she was in college. That's right. Maybe. Well, it didn't matter. If her big brothers couldn't be here to help, the least he could do was step in. After all, he could do big brother if he had to.

CHAPTER THREE

There were worse things in life than having Jack Preston carry her equipment around for a wedding shoot. As a matter of fact, having a good-looking guy in a tux as a photography assistant could probably only give Marilyn an even better reputation than she already had.

The last of the outdoor shots were filmed without a single delay or dropped camera bag. Instead of sitting in a pew like a guest, Jack had insisted on continuing to help carry her camera bag as she scurried around the church for best shots of the bride before, during, and leaving the ceremony.

The majority of guests had left the church for the beloved cocktail hour while Siobhan once again lined everyone up for family photos. The only hitch, the bridal party off to one side were having a party of their own. One of the grooms produced a bottle of tequila. Just what this party needed. *Not*. Siobhan sighed.

As the wedding party huddled around the person pouring the tequila, Jack stepped closer and leaning in as she adjusted her camera, softly whispered, "Looks like the party is starting early."

His breath skittered across her ear and she resisted the urge to swipe at the side of her face. The sensation hadn't been annoying, just unexpected. More like something one of her brothers might do to irritate her—sort of.

Grabbing her mind away from the odd feeling still tickling the side of her face, she refocused on the job at hand, staring down at the shots she'd just taken of the bride, groom, and someone's great granny. Perfect and done. Taking one step away from the altar steps, she called up to the bride. "That's the end of the list you gave me. Any last-minute extras?"

The bride and groom shook their heads.

"Great. See you at the reception hall." Heaving a long sigh, phase one was done. So far so good. She couldn't help but think climbing up a tree for the perfect nature shot was way easier than corralling wedding parties and their families. Yes, the money was nice, but there was more to life than money. All she needed was one good break and she wouldn't have to coral tipsy wedding guests anymore. She sure hoped either her sister's connection with the gallery owner or the entries for the State Fair in the fall—or both—would help. Stretching her shoulders, she turned to Jack. "Looks like we're done here."

Jack had been holding the extra camera equipment, but his gaze was on his date for the night and the shot glass being passed around. "Does this happen a lot?"

Not for her. "I don't do that many weddings, but this is the first wedding where everyone in the entourage started the party before they've even left the church."

"I've partied hard at many a wedding, but not usually this soon."

Siobhan chuckled. "I remember."

A crease between Jack's brows deepened.

"Chase's wedding?" she reminded him. "You, Kyle, and a bunch of your friends had Chase up on a chair and were carrying him around the hall while singing the Aggie fight song."

A lazy smile replaced the frown. "Oh, yeah. That *was* fun."

Siobhan shook her head. CJ had thrown a fit when she saw what the rowdy guy pals were doing, but it was the Governor who, with a single tap of his cane on the floor and the words, "We would prefer the groom in one piece for his honeymoon," had the group setting the groom back on the floor.

"Does look like someone needs to corral the bridal party or they'll miss the real fun." Jack sighed. "I'll see you at the reception."

Siobhan nodded, studying him as he walked away. How long had it been since she'd seen him? With her brothers married off one by one, Jack wasn't around as much. And who was his date? Connie seemed to be more interested in partying with her friends than hanging with her date. *Interesting.* For her, Jack had always been like an extra brother, and she was more than happy for the help, date or no date.

Her equipment loaded in the car, she hurried to the reception. She'd be expected to take photos of the bride and groom outside of the historical venue in front of their rented white Bentley before the grand entrance.

A few minutes later, she'd pulled up to the reception hall and to her surprise, Jack and Connie were out front with the bride and groom, waiting for her. Once again, Jack was helping carry things about. This reception phase of the wedding would be so much easier. No more staged photos, it would just be Siobhan, her camera and her lenses, running from one end of the hall to the other.

"I've got it from here." She hefted a smaller camera bag over her shoulder as the bride and groom made their way into the waiting room.

"You sure?" Jack raised a single brow.

"I'm sure." Maybe.

The next couple of hours whizzed by. Every so often, she'd glance up and see Jack and Connie dancing, but mostly, Connie seemed to be dancing and laughing with her friends, a glass of champagne in hand, while Jack sat at the table chatting with another of the plus-ones.

The cake cut and the clock ticking, the party was winding down and Siobhan was more than ready to call it a night. Hefting the larger camera bag over her shoulder, she blew out a slow breath. Just a little while longer and she could make a nice cup of tea and crawl into bed.

"Need anything else?" Jack's deep timbre drifted over her shoulder.

Had his voice always been so…soothing? "Actually, can I use your muscles one more time?"

His brows rose high on his forehead.

Just like earlier when he'd said he was all hers, she realized she could have found a less suggestive way of asking for his help. "I only need my one camera for the last shots of the night, but I'd like to load most of my equipment in my car so I can just head out when we're finished. You could save me a few trips if you don't mind helping me lug the rest of this gear to my car."

"Your wish is my command, Siobhan."

In half the time it would have taken her, he lifted all her spare equipment into his arms and turned toward the parking lot. Tossing a pleasant grin in her direction, he started walking. The one small bag on her shoulder, it suddenly hit her that staring at the man's posterior was so not appropriate. After all, he was like a brother. Wasn't he?

Jack really wished he could have offered to take Siobhan home. He didn't like the idea of the kid driving all the way to the ranch at this hour, but Connie was his responsibility and if he didn't get her out of here soon, he was going to be carrying his plus-one out of the place.

After he'd finished loading the photography gear in Siobhan's car and returned to the reception, it took a few minutes to spot his date for the night. Once again, Connie stood at the bar, dancing in place, with a fresh drink in her hand. The woman was going to have one hell of a hangover tomorrow, but at least she'd had a good time tonight. He put his hands on her shoulder and turned her away from the bar. "Time to go home."

"But the party isn't over."

Thankfully, the slurred words had no sooner left her mouth than the DJ announced for everyone to line up outside and bid the happy newlyweds bon voyage. Dancing her way more than walking, moving forward was slow going.

By the time they gathered her purse and shawl, and he'd wrestled the half-full glass of wine out of her hand, the bride and groom were driving away and the guests were dispersing. They meandered through the parking lot while Jack kept a tight grip on her arm.

"It was a nice wedding," she practically cooed, zig zagging beside him.

"Very nice." He tugged her closer in an effort to keep her from wandering off, relieved to finally make it to his car. Hitting the fob to unlock the passenger side, he held the door open. "Climb in."

She spun towards him, wobbling in place. "You're a good guy, Jack."

"I'm glad you think so." At this rate, he wasn't going to get her home till sunup. "Let's get in the car."

Bobbing her head nonstop, she flopped into the passenger seat and briefly fumbled with the safety belt.

"Here." He leaned over her. "I'll do that."

The buckle securely snapped in place, she smiled up at him. Not her normal sultry smile, but a goofy grin that made her look like a cartoon character. The woman was definitely three sheets to the wind.

Her door closed, he rounded the hood and noticed a shadow standing amongst the cars down a few rows. Wasn't that where Siobhan was parked? Leaving Connie safely strapped into his car, he walked over to the shadow. "Siobhan?"

Turning slowly, she looked up at him. "Hi."

"Car trouble?"

Heaving a heavy sigh, she nodded. "Car won't start. The lights come on, and the radio works, so it's not the battery."

"Do you have gas?" He made his way around to the front of her car.

She rolled her eyes and threw one hand on her hip. "Yes, I have gas. A full tank." Nibbling on her lower lip, she glanced at the car then back to Jack. "I considered looking under the hood for a loose something or other, but all my brothers ever taught me was how to drive a car, not how to fix it."

That pretty much summed up Jack's knowledge of auto

mechanics in a nutshell. "Let's take a look and see if anything jumps out at us."

Nodding her head, she inched closer to him.

Popping the hood open, he wiggled the battery cables just in case that had something to do with her problems, and then looked for any signs of leaks. Nothing stood out. "I don't see anything troublesome. Could be your starter."

Siobhan groaned.

"Have you called someone to come get you?"

"Can't. My cell phone died. I forgot to charge it."

He slammed the hood shut and dusted off his hands. "No sense in dragging anyone out at this hour. I'll give you a lift home."

"The ranch is out of your way. I'm sure the Governor won't mind."

"Nonsense. It's almost midnight. The Governor is probably sound asleep."

Lips pressed tightly together, he could see the wheels turning. No doubt she was debating what was the worse fate, accepting a ride from him or waking her grandfather up in the middle of the night. "I guess you're right."

"Good."

Bringing her camera bags with them. He tossed them into his trunk. Connie had leaned her head against the window and her snores drifted from the car.

Siobhan tilted her head, staring at Connie a moment before turning back to him. "Long day?"

Holding the back door open for her, he shrugged. "Long enough."

"Is she okay?"

"Nothing that a gallon of water and a good night's sleep won't cure."

The moment the back door slammed shut, Connie stirred, righting herself. "Are we home?"

Jack climbed into the driver's seat. "Not yet."

"I appreciate the ride." Siobhan smiled at Connie.

Her eyes open wider than they'd been in hours, Connie twisted in her seat. "Who are you?"

"Siobhan. The photographer."

Connie frowned. "Why are you in my car?"

"She's in my car," Jack corrected. "And she happens to be my best friend's kid sister, so we're taking her home."

Eyebrows lifted a little higher, Connie leaned back, twisting to better see Siobhan before settling forward again, and flopping back against the seat, shaking her head. "Doesn't look like much of a kid to me."

Backing the car out of the space, Jack looked up at the rearview mirror, his gaze meeting Siobhan's. The kid was holding back a chuckle. Her eyes sparkling and her lips plump in a rosy sheen, he had to agree, she really didn't look like a kid.

CHAPTER FOUR

"Are you sure you don't want to drop me off first and then circle back to drop off your girlfriend?"

"Not my girlfriend. I was just a plus-one." He pulled into a parking space in front of a well-manicured townhouse. "And the sooner she gets into her own bed, the better for her."

Considering that the woman had fallen back asleep as soon as Jack pulled out of the parking lot at the reception hall, and hadn't woken up since, Siobhan couldn't argue with him. As for the girlfriend mistake, she should have realized that players like Jack didn't settle for one girl. He probably had a different date every night of the week. Heaven knows before her brothers met their wives, they rotated women more often than she brushed her teeth.

The car door open, Jack unsnapped Connie's seat belt and tried to coax her awake.

"Need some help?"

He handed Siobhan a small clutch. "Find her keys for me, please."

With only a cell phone and lipstick in her purse, finding the keys was easy. "Here you go."

"Thanks. If you want to climb into the front seat, I'll be back shortly." In an effortless maneuver, Jack had Connie out of the car and in his arms. The way he managed to unlock her front door and kick it open without putting Connie down had Siobhan thinking this wasn't the first time he'd carried a woman into her, or his, house.

To her surprise, only a few minutes later Jack was

bouncing down the two front steps and climbing into the car.

"Home for you now." Jack slid into the car.

"Thank you again, Jack. I know this is out of your way."

His gaze took her in. "I'm glad to help."

"I could have called the Governor, or Mitch, he's in town this weekend."

Jack shook his head. "Pick a man in your family, any one of them would have my head next time I was at the ranch."

Pressing her lips tightly together, she tried not to laugh. "So we're talking self-preservation?"

"Absolutely." He pulled away from the curb and tossed a sly smile in her direction. "My mama did not raise a stupid boy."

"No," she leaned back, "I don't suppose she did."

"You must be exhausted." Eyes on the road, Jack changed lanes. Like her brother Kyle, his best friend clearly had a lead foot.

"Yeah. The family paid extra for photography to stay until the couple left." She tipped her head back and let her eyelids drift closed. "I really appreciated your help."

"Glad I was able to make a difference."

A second away from telling him not as glad as she was, her stomach let out a loud rumble in protest of all work and no dinner.

"Did you eat anything tonight?"

Her hand on her stomach, willing the unruly organ to be quiet, she shook her head. "Too busy. And honestly, I wasn't really hungry."

"That rumbling in your stomach says otherwise." He looked at the dashboard clock. "We'll stop for a bite. Got a preference?"

"It's bad enough I'm taking you so far out of your way." She put a hand on his arm. "I'll get something at the ranch. Hazel always has leftovers in the fridge."

He glanced down at her hand and then up into her eyes. A hint of strength and tenderness glistened in his gaze and made her go a little soft. Like her brothers, under that work hard play hard demeanor was a sweet man. Of course, as much a part of the Baron family as her brothers, he probably saw her as a little sister to be protected.

"Burgers? Chicken? What strikes your fancy?" he asked.

"You don't have to… oh, look." She pointed at the massive yellow sign down the road. "Sonic. I love their Chicago chili cheese dogs."

His smile softened and he seemed to stare at her for a fraction longer than a casual glance before putting on his turn signal.

Reflexively, her hand lifted to her face, feeling her nose and cheeks. "Do I have something on my face?"

"Excuse me?"

"Never mind." Now didn't she sound like a dumb kid.

The drive-in slots at the carhop chain were all empty save one other car. He pulled into a space nearest the front door.

"Want anything else besides the hot dog?" He read the panel by the driver door, then turned to Siobhan.

"I haven't eaten here for a while. Let me see." She unfastened the seat belt and leaned over him to better see the menu panel. "I'll have the Chicago chili cheese dog, a side order of onion rings—no, wait, make that tater tots—and a…. banana pudding milk shake."

Back in her seat, Jack stared at her again with that same confused expression. "Sure you don't want the onion rings too, or maybe a banana split?"

Now he was teasing her. "I have a healthy appetite."

"So I noticed." A broad smile stretched across his face as he turned to place her order and added a banana pudding milkshake for himself.

Shaking her head at him, she shifted to lean against the door and face him. For the first time ever, she looked at Jack. Really looked at him. No wonder her sister Eve had often used Jack as her plus-one and gold-digging-man repellant. Between sparkling blue eyes, a smile that could melt snow in Alaska, and all-around magazine cover good looks, like her brothers, under all the bravado was a nice, thoughtful guy. Who knew?

Siobhan's scent lingered in Jack's nose. She'd leaned right over his lap. Her hair had been inches from his face as she read the menu. An aroma of vanilla and almond wafted around her. Fresh, sweet, and way more intoxicating than he'd expected. With her profile direct in his line of vision, there was no missing the adorable face. Not a lick of makeup on, the natural look should have emphasized her youth; instead she looked radiant. How different from the woman he'd started the night with. Maybe it was a Baron thing. Her sister Eve wasn't big on makeup either, and even when she did wear some, it was never obvious. He'd always thought Eve was a natural beauty, but staring at Siobhan for those few moments, he had to admit, the kid had grown into quite the stunner.

"Is that a problem?" Her voice pulled him from his wandering thoughts.

"Is what a problem?"

"My healthy appetite."

No, it wasn't a problem. He'd been surprised at her enthusiasm over a sloppy hot dog. Most of the women he knew would barely pick at a salad in front of him. He found her lack of pretense refreshing. "Not at all."

The food came quickly. The only thing missing from the young server's 1950s carhop uniform was the roller skates. Jack handed Siobhan her hot dog then the tots and the drink. Taking his time unwrapping the straw for his milkshake, he watched her balancing the food on her lap and set the tall drink on the dashboard. Slowly, she unwrapped the hot dog as if it were a treasure and dug in the way he would dig into a ribeye.

"We can get back on the road if you want. I promise I won't make a mess in your car." To prove her point, she took a big bite out of the sloppy hot dog, moaned with delight, popped the tip of her tongue out to lick away a drop of chili and then smiled up at him. "See?"

Tucking his shake into the cup holder, he smiled back. "No hurry."

"Jack." Somehow she'd turned his single syllable name into a two-syllable drawl. Not quite Irish, not quite Texas, but he kind of liked it. "It's probably past your bedtime. I know it's way past mine." She took another bite of the hot dog and chewing, held her hand in front of her mouth, muttering, "Sorry, this is so good."

"Glad you're enjoying it."

She swallowed and took a hard sip of the milkshake. "I am, thank you, but it's a long drive to the ranch from here and even longer back to your place."

The idea of simply watching her devour her late-night meal with such gusto held more appeal than it should have, but Siobhan was probably dead to the world. Starting the car, he backed out of the spot. Traffic was unusually light, and he had to fight the urge to watch her more than the road.

Siobhan took the last bite of her hot dog and sighed. "That was amazing as always. Thanks for stopping, Jack."

"My pleasure."

Tossing all the trash into the paper sack, she set the bag at her feet and reached for the radio, flipping through stations. "Ooh. This song is great." She turned up the sound. A few moments later, she was rapping along to an Eminem tune. Though most people might not call her misguided efforts rapping.

"You like Eminem?"

"I do this song."

"That song came out eons ago. I don't think you were even born yet."

She blinked at him. "Not that it matters but I was most definitely already born when this song first came out. But the reason I know the song is because it's one of my mother's favorites."

It took him a moment to process that the kid was not a kid at all, but a fully legal adult by more than a few years. When the heck had that happened?

Rap was not his favorite form of music, but as cute as Siobhan looked bobbing her head to the song, she was truly and rightfully butchering the tune. That unbridled exuberance was the kid he remembered. He could probably watch her for hours. There was no worry over how she appeared to others. Definitely a Baron through and through. But right now he had precious cargo to get home to her family.

For the rest of the ride to the ranch, she flipped from station to station and head bobbing, sang along to different tunes. Disappointment actually made itself at home in the pit of his stomach when he reached the family ranch and pulled into the long driveway.

"We're here." Siobhan sat up straight. As soon as the car came to a stop, she hopped out before he could come around and open her door. "You have a long drive back to your condo. You don't need to stick around."

"Sorry, kid. I always see a lady to her door." The ranch was most likely the safest place for miles, but driving away with a woman standing on her doorstep was not an option for him, never mind when the woman in question was the baby sister of his best friend.

A light burned in the front window and he saw movement. A moment later, the front door swung open. Siobhan's grandmother smiled. "Jack Preston. What a nice surprise." Her gazed drifted over his shoulder to his car and then narrowing slightly, she looked at Siobhan. "What happened to your car?"

"It wouldn't start and Jack was there so he offered a ride."

"In that case." She stepped back from the door. "Thank you, Jack, for driving Siobhan. Please come in."

The thought of politely refusing crossed his mind, but he'd been a part of the Baron household long enough to know when Lila Baron gave instructions, it was best to do as you were told. "Thank you, but only a moment, I have a long drive still."

"Nonsense." Lila closed the door behind them. "You're staying with us. As you've already pointed out, it's late and you have a long drive."

"Grams is right. You know we have more spare rooms than a Baron hotel."

Jack's gaze bounded from Siobhan to her grandmother. He knew when he was outnumbered. "I guess I'm staying." The question at hand now was why did the idea of waking up with the Barons—especially one Baron—hold so much appeal? More so, how much trouble would that appeal get him into?

CHAPTER FIVE

nyone would think after eating as much as Siobhan had before going to bed that she'd still be stuffed to the gills. Nope, she was ravenous as usual. One bite of Hazel's from scratch blueberry pancakes and her eyes closed in sheer delightful appreciation. By the time the three of them last night had chatted a bit about the wedding and car rescue and her grandmother had set Jack up with a bed and a change of clothing for the morning, she was now running on only four hours of sleep and in desperate need of a gallon of coffee.

"Didn't they feed you last night?" The Governor sat at one end of the table. "Slow down, girl. Breakfast isn't a race."

Siobhan wiped her mouth and put down her napkin. "Yes, sir."

"I hear Jack had to bring you home." Mitch stood at the buffet pouring himself a glass of orange juice.

"My car broke down." She turned to her grandfather. "Which reminds me. We're going to have to get the car fixed or towed before the hall notices it's still there."

"Already taken care of." The Governor looked to the doorway where Hazel carried a full pot of hot coffee.

"Bless you." Siobhan smiled up at the family housekeeper who circled the table, filling the empty coffee cups before setting the pot down on the warmer on the buffet.

"So where is our knight in shining armor?" Mitch took a sip of his hot brew.

"Ready for one of Hazel's scrumptious breakfasts." Jack appeared in the dining room freshly showered and dressed. For as long as Siobhan could remember, her brothers and Jack swapped clothes like a couple of teenage girls. Having them all the same size had made impromptu sleepovers a piece of cake.

A well-raised Texas boy, Jack stopped first to shake the Governor's hand, then circled to the other side and kissed Grams on the cheek the same way any of the family would have.

"It was our good fortune you were at the wedding to rescue our girl." Grams grinned up at Jack as if he were one of her own precious grandchildren. The scene brought a smile to her face.

He chose the seat next to her and swiftly unfolded the cloth napkin across his lap. "I was a last-minute plus-one. Glad I was there. I hate to think how long she'd have been stuck there." His gaze met hers and she recognized the silent reproof in his eyes. She could read this man as well as any of her brothers and knew as sure as her name was Siobhan Pegeen Baron that the momentary stern glare was in reference to her dead cell phone.

With a short nod of her head, she let him know 'message received' and dug into her pancakes again.

"Not the best of neighborhoods." Mitch shook his head. "We appreciate you stepping in."

"Nothing y'all wouldn't have done."

No one could argue with that. All her brothers and cousins were raised to be gentlemen. Old-fashioned chivalry was alive and well in this part of Texas. Even the players in the family were respectful and protective of the women in their lives. No matter how well they did or didn't know them. Jack was part of the family and, of course, he would make sure she was safe. The same way he took care of getting his own date home safe and sound. But, like the rest of her family, she was very, very glad that Jack had been there.

"Did you have a good time at the wedding?" Grams asked him.

"Actually, I had more fun helping Siobhan."

"How's that?" Mitch lifted his gaze from his plate to

Siobhan then back to Jack.

"You all know I was replacing Marilyn as principal photographer but the assistant she hired never showed up."

Jack raised his hand. "Meet her temporary assistant."

"Wasn't that sweet of you?" Grams grinned from ear to ear. As if showing their appreciation, Honey, the border collie at her grandmother's side, lifted her head from the floor and began swishing her tail.

Listening to Jack retell the events of the night from his perspective as impromptu photography assistant had Mitch staring back and forth intently at both of them. Though there was no reason for it, his scrutiny had her wanting to shift in her seat.

"Siobhan did a great job." Jack snagged a slice of toast off of a platter. "The way she coaxed just the right expressions and reactions from the bridal party was impressive. Not an easy feat to corral everyone for the photos when quite a few were already drunk."

"Oh, my." Her grandmother pointed to a framed print of one of her Big Bend photos that hung across the room, a smile taking over her face again. "She is quite the photographer."

Jack turned his head, his gaze narrowed as he studied the photograph, then whistled. "That's a lot of talent."

"Thank you." She smiled up at him, thankful for the support.

"Weddings are just a side gig. Help pay the bills until I can make a name for myself." The wedding gigs had actually been fun, but her first love was definitely her wildlife photography and her action photos like the Baroness racing next. Most of her childhood she'd dreamed of either captaining racing yachts or photo journalism.

Her cell phone played "Irish Eyes" and a smile tugged hard at the corners of her mouth. The most difficult part of having an Irish mother and an American father was splitting her time between the two. She loved them both so much, but it was increasingly looking like her life was unfolding here more than across the pond, so hearing her mother's voice always made her smile. "It's Mum. She probably wants to hear how the wedding went. Is it all right if I put her on speakerphone?"

"No phone at the table is a rule that can always be broken for Maura." The Governor smiled sincerely and Siobhan tapped at her phone. Could this morning get any better?

"Hi Mum. You're on speaker." Siobhan's eyes lit up.

Though he tried his best to be discreet, Jack couldn't help but watch her.

"Hello to everyone." A chorus of hello, hi, and good morning echoed around the room. "Tell me, girl, how was the wedding yesterday?" Her mother's musical lilt came through the phone.

A wide grin on her face, Siobhan leaned back in her seat and began recounting the events in more detail than before. With each story of the night, Siobhan's enthusiasm grew. Practically bouncing in her chair, her smile bloomed and her eyes sparkled. Her love for her mother seemed to energize her every sentence. The same could be said for her mother. Jack didn't listen to the words, but the tone. In every question her mother asked, the pride in her voice couldn't be missed.

The delight in Siobhan's voice and her sweet relationship with her mother washed over him. She looked downright adorable. Though he was pretty sure Siobhan would give him an earful if she heard him think that. Grown up or not, her smile was infectious. No way could he watch her excitement and not smile back.

When the call was over, Siobhan gave a wistful sigh before digging back into her food.

"Your mother sounds good." The Governor sipped his coffee with one hand and scratched behind Moon's ears with the other. Honey's littermate leaned into the Governor's leg. Those two dogs were as lucky as the rest of the Baron clan.

"I worry about her all alone sometimes, but it's good to hear all is well."

And wasn't that the icing on the cake. Not only did the kid like her mother, she worried about her too.

"Governor?" Siobhan wiped the corners of her mouth with her napkin. "I was planning to hit the mall today. There are a few things I need to pick up at the camera store. Since I don't have my car, may I borrow one of the other ones?"

"I can take you." The words slipped out before Jack had time to think better of it.

Eyes wide, Siobhan's gaze raced back to his. "You don't need to go out of your way again."

The way Mitch and the Governor's attention had whipped around to him, he almost thought twice about his offer, but instead, his mouth kicked into gear before his brain could stop him. "I need to stop at the mall also. Today is as good as any."

"Are you sure you don't mind?"

His gaze casually took in the additional sets of eyes staring at him. What the heck, it was just a ride to the mall, he wasn't asking for the kid's hand in marriage. "I'm sure."

"Then I guess I don't need a car after all." Siobhan pushed to her feet. "Give me two minutes to grab my purse and I'll meet you at the front door."

Containing the urge to smile back as brightly as she was, Jack nodded.

Siobhan bounced out of the room, her absence leaving a vacuum. He dared to look at the others at the table. He couldn't swear to it, but he thought he saw a glimmer of suspicion in Mitch's gaze. Same with the Governor. Shaking his imagination clear, he stood. He had to be reading into their expressions. Siobhan was just a kid and he was just helping out a friend's little sister. Walking to the other end of the table, he kissed Lila again. "Thank you for your hospitality."

"Thank you for rescuing our girl." The older woman smiled up at him again.

"My pleasure." Nodding at the Governor, he turned,

noticing Mitch was no longer seated. He found Siobhan's brother at the front door, a stern expression directed at him. Jack stopped a few feet from him.

"Our baby sister thinks she's all grown up."

Jack nodded.

"Just so we're clear."

Again, he bobbed his head. He knew better than anyone that not all that long ago he was partying hardy with Kyle and the others while Siobhan was still in pigtails and braces. So why had he not let her use one of the other ranch cars?

Siobhan appeared at the top of the steps, her purse over her shoulder and a baseball hat in her hand. She bounced down the stairs. "Ready?"

"Your carriage awaits." Holding the door open with one hand, he waved her outside and ignored the way Mitch continued to watch them.

Buckled in, he put the car in gear and resisted the urge to chuckle as she plopped the baseball hat on, backwards. Reaching for the radio, she fiddled with the stations until she found one she liked, then twisted to face him. "So, what are you needing at the mall?"

Scrambling quickly, he ran through his to-do list, thrilled to remember his mother's birthday was coming up. "I need a gift."

Her head tipped to one side. "Oh."

"Promise not to laugh?"

She nodded.

"Mom's birthday is coming up and I haven't a clue what to get her. Frankly, I could use a little input of the feminine persuasion."

"Cool." She twisted around and leaned back in place. "I'm great at old lady shopping."

He knew his brows had just shot up high. "Uh, just don't say that to my mother. She still refuses to consider herself middle-aged."

She kicked her head back and laughed. "Got it."

"Your mother seems really nice."

"Oh, that she is. When God handed out mothers, I won the lottery. She's always been a huge support. When people tell me that I should settle down and get a real job, Mum was the first to tell me to ignore the naysayers and follow my dream. Even though I get to talk to her all the time, it's not quite the same as having her here to share a cuppa with or just get a hug. I really wish she were closer to share in all the things happening. But she's become the most requested wedding coordinator in the county, getting away isn't easy for her. I know she loves what she does, but I really do think she's happy I'm here in Texas following my dreams."

"That picture in the dining room really is wonderful."

"Thank you. The goal is to turn my love of photography into a lucrative career. It's not quite the same as an engineering or accounting degree, but I'm entered in the State Fair and hoping to get some recognition to one day have a photography showing. There's a woman who owns a small gallery in the arts district. She's a friend of Paige's and really liked my work. She suggested if I can get some formal recognition, she'd be willing to hang some of my work the next time she does a show of up-and-coming artists."

"That's great."

Her shoulders hunched up, her smile widened and her eyes sparkled. "I know. I haven't told anyone yet, you know, just in case. Not even Mum, and I usually tell her everything."

"If I've learned anything watching you since last night, it's that you have talent." And spunk, he thought. "I'm sure you can make it work."

"I hope so." A peppy tune came on the radio and she nearly sprung from the seat. "Oh, I love this song."

Next thing he knew, the windows were down on her side of the car, and her fingers were snapping in time to the music. With her arms up in the air, she bopped to the beat, pretty much dancing in her seat. On top of that she was singing at the top of her lungs, though she couldn't sing worth a damn, but he didn't seem to care. Once again the word adorable came to mind, along with Mitch's parting words. *Our baby sister thinks she's all grown up.* Baby sister. Every instinct he had screamed back off, walk away.

But whether Mitch liked it or not, this free spirit was most definitely not a baby anymore. And whether he liked it or not, at the top of the best friend Bro Code, in big bold letters, little sisters were off limits. Which left one question: what the heck was he getting himself into?

CHAPTER SIX

"Do you have any ideas about what to buy?" Siobhan unsnapped her seatbelt.

Jack clicked the fob on his key ring and locked the car with a beep. "I have no ideas. I hadn't thought too hard about it, hoping inspiration would strike me."

The mall was crawling with people, it was a miracle they found a parking spot so close to the doors.

"Is she like Gram and the Governor, buys what she wants when she wants it, or does she have a long list of things she wants but no time to shop for?"

He fell into step beside her. "Is a little of both a helpful answer?"

"Only if you have a list of what she hasn't bought herself?"

"And that's the rub. I freely admit if she mentioned anything, I didn't pay attention."

Siobhan blew out a huffy breath and muttered, "Men." Inside she thought back to the time or two she'd met Jack's parents at a gathering at the ranch. Mrs. Preston had struck her as rather down to earth, well dressed, but not overly dressed, and always smiling. Mr. Preston seemed to like his cigars and bourbon with the rest of the older men. "Does she have a favorite clothing store?"

Frowning, Jack pressed his lips and seemed to be considering the question. "I think I've seen her come home with shopping bags from Chico's. Does that sound right?"

"It does." Siobhan smiled. She'd thought his mom was practical. "And there's a shop here in the mall too."

Halfway across the mall, the ground floor pavilion had

a model train store that had set up a massive display. The line of mothers and children to get in and see the trains was trailing down the side and around a corner. She and Jack had just reached the storefront when Siobhan noticed a woman exiting with an infant on her hip, a two or three year old gripped tightly and another kid running ahead.

"Josiah, get back here!" the frazzled woman shouted as loudly as she'd dared in public.

The kid stopped in his tracks and looked back at his mother, now struggling to open one of the many folded strollers that had been parked outside the storefront.

"At least he stopped." Siobhan kept her eye on the harried mom.

"What?" Jack stopped beside her.

"Hold on a sec." Scurrying the few feet to where the woman was still trying to balance a baby, and with her free hand both coral a toddler and open the stroller. "May I help you?"

"Oh, lord, yes." The poor woman looked as though she hadn't slept in a month of Sundays. Her hair up in a messy bun, what looked like a ketchup stain, probably from the kid's lunch, was prominently displayed on the left breast pocket of her shirt. "I knew not bringing my husband was going to be a problem."

The next thing Siobhan knew, instead of stepping out of the way to allow her to open the stroller, the woman, without a second's hesitation, dropped the baby in her arms. Within seconds the fussy baby had stopped crying and large blue eyes studied her with intense curiosity.

"Well, aren't you a sweetie." She absolutely loved babies, and most of them knew it. The mom was lucky she hadn't handed the kid off to someone uncomfortable around babies. Wiggling her fingers in front of the baby, she managed to coax a wide smile. "Atta girl. Are we having a good time?"

Behind her, the mom had managed to open the double stroller, snap the toddler into the back seat, and had placed the older sons hands firmly on the handle of the stroller with strict instructions not to move an inch or there'd be no ice cream for dessert tonight.

Siobhan liked the woman's style.

"I can't tell you how much I appreciate the help." Mom held her arms out to the baby, and to everyone's surprise, she frowned and leaned into Siobhan.

That coaxed a smile out of Siobhan. "Well, I like you too."

The mother stood, her hands on her hips, and her eyebrows high. "I'll be. She normally doesn't cotton to strangers. You either have kids of your own or the magic touch."

"My mother often says we've been blessed by the leprechauns. We like babies and babies like us."

"I've never heard it put that way, but I'd have to agree." Once again the mother clapped her hands lightly and then stretched them out to the baby.

At the same moment, the older boy seemed to see his chance to slip past his mother's watchful eye, and carefully eased one hand away from the stroller.

Jack squatted down. "Are you going somewhere?"

The little boy shook his head and quickly grabbed the stroller handle again with his wayward hand.

A smile on his face, Jack nodded. "I bet you're a good big brother. You help your mom with your little brother and sister, don't you?"

The silent child nodded and a second later decided he wasn't in trouble and smiled. By now the mom had retrieved the baby, latched her into the front of the stroller, and taking her place behind the older boy, smiled up at them. "I cannot thank both of you enough. Y'all are going to be great parents someday."

"Oh, we're not..." Jack started, but the woman was already making her way to the mall exit.

"Back to your mother's gift." She turned and looked at Jack who to her surprise was studying her much like he'd done last night when she thought she might have something on her face.

Blinking, Jack nodded. "Right."

Siobhan marched toward his mother's favorite store, her

mind lingering on the sweet baby smell. Why were all babies so cute? This one was cuter than a baby had a right to be. And the way Jack got down on his haunches to meet the little boy at eye level, that surprised the heck out of her. She couldn't help but wonder, what other surprises might Jack Preston have in store for her?

The image of Siobhan smiling and cooing and playing with that baby until the little girl grinned back at her would not stop replaying in his mind. The sight of her with the baby in her arms had done something to Jack. Something he couldn't explain, and didn't quite fully understand. Children were not his thing. He was an only child and the Baron clan was the closest thing to siblings and extended family for him. None of them had kids so he had limited experience with short people. And yet, somehow, watching Siobhan, he'd known that helping the mom with her wayward son meant getting down to his level.

"That was nice of you to offer to help." What he really wanted to say was she looked amazing smiling at the baby.

Walking, Siobhan shrugged. "It was the decent thing to do. Poor woman was clearly frazzled."

Decent thing to do. That's how his mama had raised him: open doors for ladies, pull out chairs for them, help them on with their jackets or cover-ups. And yet, actually doing something to help an overwhelmed mother had not occurred to him until Siobhan so seamlessly stepped in.

Her arm shot up and she pointed straight ahead. "Chico's is at the other end of the mall."

It took him a long moment to shift from the images of her and the baby to what she was saying, and another minute still to remember why they were here.

"Your mother's present. Remember?"

"Yes, sorry, my mind wandered."

"After that, we can hit the photography store. What I need will only take a minute."

To his surprise, and relief, it had taken all of ten minutes, fifteen tops, to pick out a dress that he was positive his mom would love, along with a few pieces of matching jewelry. Siobhan had headed straight for the dress on the mannequin. "This looks like your mom."

His mother was always in sleeveless dresses like that, so he had to agree. "I think you're right. She often says dresses like this are more comfortable than her pajamas."

"There you go." Siobhan picked out some subtle but substantial jewelry pieces.

He'd been less sure his mom would wear the large pieces, but Siobhan seemed convinced, and just like that, he was done shopping for his mother.

Out the door, a tie store across the way caught his eye. There were two things his dad had taught him from an early age; the best deals in life will be made on the golf course, and a man's tie says a great deal more about him than his handshake. To his father's delight, Jack had taken to both the game of golf and to ties.

Siobhan stopped in her tracks beside him. "What?"

He blinked and turned to face her. "Sorry, you might say my kryptonite is ties. I'm probably the last guy in the world under forty who loves ties. I still wear them to the office."

She cocked her head. "I have time. Let's go in."

"That won't be necessary. I need another tie like I need a hole in my head."

"Ah." Her face lit up. "It's way more fun buying something you like and don't need." Before he could stop her, she'd turned away and marched off in that direction.

Once again she had him smiling. He guessed he was buying a tie today.

A crisp and classic tie caught his attention first. Hermes, of course. Tried and true.

Siobhan looked from the tie to him and frowned. "Seriously, Jack? Could your choice be more boring?"

"Boring?" He looked down at the article in his hands. "These are the best ties on the market."

"Perhaps. But it's also staid and predictable."

"What's wrong with that? Who wants to do business with someone frivolous and unreliable?"

"For someone who played hard with my brothers, you have a lot to learn about stepping out of your comfort zone." Taking hold of his hand, she dragged him to a rack of ties with more color flashing at him than the sails on a Baron racing yacht.

He braced for impact. Sure enough, she picked up a tie with a school of neon fish blazoned front and center.

"No."

Her gaze narrowing, she studied the tie. "Okay, maybe fish isn't the real you anyhow."

Thank heavens for that. Her next choices became wilder and wilder. The sweet bouncy kid he remembered had clearly grown into a bit of a rebel. Apparently, she took after her brothers more than her sisters. He'd never seen Eve or Paige even wear a ball cap, never mind backwards. And singing in the front seat, bouncing about with the windows down? Nope, not Paige or Eve either. Now, Kyle... Lord, help whoever fell for this woman, their life together would be one helluva ride.

"Here." She thrust a tie at him that looked like paisley had dropped acid.

"Really?"

"Yes. It's wild and it will match those gray suits you probably have."

He laughed. Most of his suits were indeed gray. A few dark blue, but mostly gray because it made it easier to match shirts and ties. "No."

Rolling her eyes at him, she kept trying. "How about this one?"

For all the crazy options she'd pointed out, this one was oddly sedate in its flamboyance. Grays, blues, and reds came together in swathes with thin black lines as well. It actually didn't look that bad.

"It's a Jerry Garcia tie."

His gaze dropped to the signature and back. "As in the Grateful Dead?"

Smiling, she nodded enthusiastically.

"You like the Grateful Dead?"

She shrugged. "I like all music, but isn't the tie great?"

Who'd have thunk that a musician from the era of sex, drugs, and rock and roll would one day have a line of ties. "Actually, I kind of like it."

Her smile grew even wider. "Now, you're talking."

Apparently, he was buying a hippie tie. What would his father have to say about him now? The thought brought a smile to his face.

"What's so funny?"

"Nothing. Let's buy a tie."

Everyone in his office was going to think he'd gone crazy. Then again, here he was in a shopping mall with his best friend's little sister, having the best time buying ties. Yes, he may very well have gone completely crazy.

Siobhan had been right about more than one thing today, her stop at the camera store had taken even less time than their run through the dress shop. The funny thing was he wished he needed to shop for something else. The entire walk from the camera shop to the mall exit, while thinking on how to extend the day, he'd been making polite chit-chat about the dress, the ties, and his need to loosen up. That was a riot. His parents were trying to get him to settle down and man up and Siobhan thought he needed to loosen up.

Holding the door open for Siobhan, he'd not come up with a single reasonable excuse to extend their time together when she came to a stop in front of him. "Do you like Renaissance Festivals?"

"I suppose. Haven't been since I was a kid."

"I had plans to go tomorrow with my friend Bridget, but her mum phoned that her grandma went to hospital for emergency bypass surgery so she's flying home sooner than planned. What about you?"

"Sorry to hear that. I hope she'll be okay, but what about me?"

"Do you want to go with me?"

"Oh." His head spun at the solution to spending more time with her landing at his feet, so to speak. Another whole day? And why not? Maybe because she had four big brothers who he was pretty sure would not like the idea. An idea that was quickly growing on him. Yep, now he could confirm, he'd definitely gone completely crazy. "I'd love to."

CHAPTER SEVEN

The thought of dressing up for the Renaissance Festival in period garb had briefly crossed Siobhan's mind, but just as quickly she discarded the idea. That had been her original plan with Bridget, but this morning with Jack, the idea simply didn't feel right.

Unlike most mornings at the ranch, she was the only family member home when Jack's car pulled up to the front door. Bottle of water in hand, she flung the door open and pulling it tightly closed behind her, trotted down the steps.

"I guess you're ready to go?" Jack chuckled as she climbed into his car.

She laughed. "I love the Renaissance Festival. Wish it came to town more than once a year."

"Ah, but then the law of diminishing returns would kick in and the anticipation and fun simply wouldn't be there."

Her head fell back against the seat and she resisted the urge to roll her eyes. "Bringing up economics sounds like something my grandfather would do."

"Thank you." Jack put the car in gear and cast a cheeky grin in her direction. "I happen to like the Governor. I'll consider that a compliment."

"I like him too. Love him in fact, but I suspect the day will be more entertaining if we leave economics out of it."

This time Jack let out a deep belly laugh. "Agreed."

Asking Jack to this festival had been an impulse. The words had slipped out of her mouth before she gave herself a chance to think it through. Picking out a tie for him yesterday had been more fun than she would have expected. Not once did he treat her like the little sister of the family. Any moment she kept expecting him to stick his arm out and ruffle the top of her head the way he and her brothers would when she was still bouncing around in school uniforms. Her gut kept reminding her that he was still her brother's best friend, had always been like an extra brother; and for her not to read too much into his treating her like an equal—as if there weren't at least ten years between them. Right now, she didn't feel much like paying attention to her gut. The plan was to simply enjoy the day and the company.

The second they crossed through the makeshift gates, the medieval world surrounded them.

"Okay, this was impressive when I was a teen and it's still impressive now." Jack's gaze cut across the booths and stands and back. The twinkle in his eyes reminded her of the proverbial kid on Christmas morning.

"As much as I love the atmosphere, I'm ready for a juicy turkey leg and corn on the cob. I don't know what they do differently, but the corn here is always so darn good."

"First of all, you do realize it's only ten o'clock in the morning?" Jack held back a chuckle. "And secondly, they probably roast it instead of boiling it."

"That's what the Governor says. One of these days I'm going to try out the theory. And for the record, it's never too early for lunch."

Jack let out a deep rumbled laugh. "Sounds like a plan."

"Oh, look." Spotting the archery booth, her arm pointed straight ahead. "Care to give it a go?"

He studied her, but she couldn't read his face. "Sure. Have you done archery before?"

"A few times, maybe more. You?"

"A few times." He chuckled softly. "I can probably give you some pointers if you like."

The man had no idea what he was getting himself into. "I'll take them."

"I'll go first." Jack momentarily set his hand on her lower back and nudged her forward.

At the booth, she motioned for him to step up and choose his bow. The target field was set back beside the booth, pointing away from the crowds.

"The key is to choose the correct size bow for your strength. Bigger isn't always better."

Biting back a smile, Siobhan nodded and picked up her bow and arrows and followed Jack to the field. Since Jack was up first, she stepped aside as he nocked his arrow and let it fly. An acceptable shot, he'd hit the target center, but not a center bullseye.

Letting his bow down to his side, Jack stepped back. "Now you try."

Curious to how the pseudo-Big Brother would behave, she picked up the bow, pretending to struggle. He stepped closer to her, put his large hands on hers, and softly talked her through the motions. His breath skittered across her ear, only this time it felt nothing like an annoying tease by a big brother. A girl could get used to Jack standing close, whispering in her ear, and… oh, she wasn't going there.

The first shot barely nicked the target.

"Let's try again." Jack moved in closer, standing directly behind her, she could feel his breath on the back of her neck. Tingles skittered down her spine. Maybe this joking thing hadn't been her best idea. His arms nearly wrapped around her as his hands helped her pull back the arrow and then let it fly. The arrow landed closer to center but not close enough.

He stepped out of her space and the loss punched her smack in the gut. She had to shake off the sensation. Straightening her spine, she put on a smile and looked up at him. "You up for a wager?"

He cocked his head. "What kind of wager?"

"Whoever scores the fewest points buys lunch."

His brows rose high on his forehead and he sucked in a hissing breath. "I don't know. That feels too much like taking advantage of you."

Having learned a thing or two growing up in a competitive family, she shook her head. "What's the matter? Chicken?"

A mischievous twinkle lit his eyes. "You're on."

She stepped out of the way. "Age before beauty."

"Ha ha," he quipped. Standing in place, he went

through his quiver of arrows. All came close, but not a single one hit the bullseye straight on.

Retreating for her to take her turn, he smiled almost guiltily at her. "You'd have to hit the red circle just about every time to beat my score."

Trying really hard not to give away that he was about to be walloped, she avoided looking at him and set up her first shot. First arrow landed just inside the red dot. She didn't dare look over her shoulder at him. Second arrow landed a smidgeon closer to the inside. Jack let out a small "hmm" but she ignored him. Third arrow hit the red dot dead center.

From behind her she heard Jack mutter, "I think I've been had."

As with the three arrows before, the last two pierced dead center of the bullseye.

Grinning from ear to ear, she turned around to see Jack smiling and shaking his head. "I have most definitely been hustled."

"Me? Would I do that?" She knew she was grinning like the cat who'd swallowed the canary, but it had been so much fun to show him she was most definitely not a defenseless little kid anymore. She was most definitely very grown up. What she hadn't quite figured out was, why had that suddenly become so very important to her?

From what Jack remembered, his favorite part of the annual Renaissance Festival as a teenager had been the jousting and collecting souvenirs. He was pretty sure the caricature of him in a jester's hat was still hanging in his old room at his parents' house. What he couldn't remember from all those years ago, was having such a good time. As much as he'd love to say it was the freshness of exploring the ancient scene with adult eyes, he knew darn well the joy had been in seeing everything through Siobhan's eyes. The woman was bright, carefree, had a killer sense of humor, and yeah, she could be a little cheeky at times. No doubt something genetic she shared with her brother Kyle. But mostly, she kept Jack on his toes. Her verbal sparring was as tight as her archery skills.

He honestly couldn't remember simply enjoying a day so much with anyone. Who knew his best friend's little sister would grow up to be such an amazing person? When she was really little and visited from Ireland during summers or holiday breaks, he remembered her as a bit annoying. Always wanting to tag along, always talking, even tattling on them a time or two when they did things they weren't supposed to. Eventually she blossomed into a sweet teen. The only interest she'd had in hanging out with her brothers was on the sailboat. He remembered her holding her own helping the crew with the sails. Somewhere in the back of his mind, he had a vague memory of her beating the pants off her brothers in a game of poker. As a matter of fact, he remembered owing her about a hundred bucks from that night, and he wasn't sure if he'd ever paid her or not. For the most part, she didn't really hang around much as she usually had a girlfriend or some other kid with her. Jack had paid so little attention to the kid, that somehow he'd completely missed that she'd grown up.

They'd eaten their way across the fairgrounds, enjoyed the jousting, the marionettes, the pickles, and even the story time. For several hours, he'd practically forgotten he lived in the twenty-first century. Laden with an odd array of souvenirs, including a sword and shield, Jack put all their newly acquired trinkets into the back of his SUV.

In the car, Siobhan kicked her head back and plopped her feet on the dashboard. "I think I could sleep for a week."

"Ditto." He started the car, carefully backing out. "I haven't taken that many steps since I gave up marathons."

"I know what you mean. My feet are sooo tired."

His phone sounded and hitting the button on his steering wheel, he picked up the call. "Hey, John."

"What time you coming, man?"

Coming? He looked at the clock on the dashboard wishing the dumb thing had a calendar.

"Brats are on the grill, the water's just the right temperature, and Greg has a bonfire big enough to see from the moon."

Crap. John's birthday party was tonight. "Sorry, something came up. I'm running a bit behind."

"No problem. But if you can, pick up a couple of bags of ice. The ice maker in the house is on the fritz."

"Got it. Ice." The two men said their quick goodbyes and Jack hoped he could get away with just soaking his tired feet in the hot tub. Maybe no one would notice if he just took a nap.

"Did I mess up your plans?" Siobhan twisted in his direction, her expression heavy with concern.

"No. I forgot about my friends' birthday party."

"You have a friend other than my brothers?" she teased, the humor returning to her eyes.

He chuckled. "Yes. Believe it or not, my life does not revolve around just your family." Thankfully, she didn't call him out on spending the last three days with her.

"Does your friend live far from here?"

"Actually, he's on the way to Paradise Ridge."

"Oh." Her frown was back. "I know it's been a long day. If you want to just go to your friend's, I can get an Uber home."

"Seriously? You think I'd make you Uber home?" Had she really just said that to him? Even if she didn't have four over protective older brothers, what kind of man did she think he was?

"Sorry. I was just trying to help."

Now he felt bad for taking the sparkle from her eyes.

"There's an easy solution, if you're up to staying out a little later?"

Her face lit up as she straightened in her seat. "Always."

"Want to join me at the party?"

"I heard the words bonfire. Will there be s'mores?"

He could not stop himself from cackling out loud. "You can't possibly still be hungry?"

"I'm always hungry, but I'll come even if there aren't

any s'mores."

"Okay, then. One stop for ice and we're off to a birthday party." A few minutes ago the idea of heading to a party after such a long day held as much appeal as swimming with crocodiles in the bayou. Now, with Siobhan joining him, a long night sounded just fine.

He was starting to get used to her taking control of the radio, singing and swaying along to whatever tune she found. Even when she lowered the windows and sang loud enough to cause a scene for the cars driving by, all he could do was smile. By the time he pulled onto the double-wide circular drive at John's house, the long line of cars told him the party was in full swing.

"Hey, Jack." John slapped his friend on the back.

"John, this is Siobhan Baron."

His friend shook her hand. "Pleasure to meet you."

"You have a lovely home."

"Thanks." He turned and waved a poker across the way. "The drinks are on the table, food's over there, and there are plenty of fixings for s'mores if you're so inclined. Just go ahead and make yourselves at home, I have to tend to the fire. Excuse me."

Siobhan looked up at him, the smile on her face as wide as the Rio Grande. "S'mores."

If all it took to put that huge grin on Siobhan's face was a little chocolate covered marshmallow with graham crackers, then he would gladly buy a lifetime supply. And didn't that hold way more appeal than it should have—a lifetime with Siobhan?

CHAPTER EIGHT

Across the lawn, large flames darted upward from a lit pile of logs. There were benefits to living outside city limits with no close neighbors. From nearby speakers, music played and Siobhan danced toward the fire much the way she bounced to the tunes in his car.

"Love a woman with rhythm." His friend Eddie, who had clearly started partying a long while ago, grabbed her hand and spun her around, his feet twisting around in such a way that Jack expected him to fall flat on his face any second.

And if the man didn't let go of Siobhan sooner than that, Jack just might help Eddie hit the dirt.

For the first time, Jack noticed a sharp similarity in Siobhan with her sisters. The fun-loving, carefree young woman had stiffened ever so slightly. She smiled politely at Eddie. The same plastic smile that Jack had seen on every socialite he'd ever had to spend a fundraising evening with. Siobhan's simple words of, *thank you for the dance*, as she backed away reminded him of the same graceful demeanor her older sisters had used when dispatching an unwanted suitor. Not till this very second did he realize there were two sides to Siobhan Baron, and the one he was looking at right now was very much grown up.

"Just one more dance," Eddie slurred.

"Sorry, pal." Jack did his best to plaster on the same polite smile rather than shove his tipsy friend across the field with a single blow. "My turn." Her hand in his, he spun Siobhan in the opposite direction and then twirling her again and again, had successfully moved her a safe distance from Eddie. Coming to a stop, still holding her hand, he slightly shook his head. "Sorry about that. Eddie sometimes doesn't know when to stop."

"Seems more like he doesn't know when to start either." Her gaze darted over his shoulder at his friend. "It's early but I get the feeling he's been drinking for a while. What's he trying to drown away?"

Jack nodded his head, intrigued by her insight. "A few months ago his girlfriend, the one he'd bought a ring for, decided that she'd rather date a man with more zeros in his bank account so she broke up with him and made a play for John."

"Ouch."

"Yeah. That about covers it. He's been drowning his sorrows ever since. If he doesn't snap out of it on his own, we may find ourselves doing a good old-fashioned intervention."

A peppy but more mellow tune kicked in and still holding her hand, Jack pulled her in a little closer. "May I have this dance, Miss?"

"Why, I'd be delighted, kind sir." Siobhan's effort at a thick southern accent came out more like a muddled Irish brogue and almost made him laugh.

Instead, they swayed to the rhythm as if this wasn't the first time they'd danced together. A lot about the last few days felt like they'd been friends for years. Had he ever felt that way about a woman? He almost shook his head, answering his own thoughts. Women were never friends, just companions, and they never had him wishing the night together would never end.

"Ooh." Siobhan eased back, slowing her movements. "They're carrying a tray of s'mores fixings to the fire."

Jack didn't know if he wanted to laugh at her enthusiasm over s'mores, or cry at the loss of contact. Both of which gave him reason to think twice about what was happening with Siobhan Baron. The next thing he knew, he had a stick in his hand with a fat marshmallow on the tip, dangling near the fire.

"I seriously love s'mores." Sitting beside him, she twirled her stick about. "The secret is to tan the marshmallow evenly around without letting it burn."

He felt the corners of his mouth tilt up in another smile. "The Siobhan method of s'mores building?"

"I'll have you know, I am the best s'mores maker in the entire Baron clan."

"The best?" He lowered his tone.

"Your friend Kyle is so dang inpatient that he always lets it catch fire and burn." She continued turning the stick like a rotisserie chicken. "And Craig, he's just as bad, but Mitch, he's the opposite. When he would do s'mores, the marshmallows are usually lily white when he pulls them off. I wouldn't be surprised if the middles are still cold."

"How long do you hold it to the fire?"

"Depends on how you like it." She glanced at his marshmallow. "I'd say yours is perfect."

He pulled it away from the fire and stared at the thing. It had been so many years since he'd done this that he'd forgotten not to touch the hot marshmallow with his fingers. It had only taken a second of skin on sugar to realize that using his hands was not the best of ideas.

"Here." She handed him her stick to hold, then placing a slab of chocolate on a graham cracker, she quickly sandwiched the two crackers around his marshmallow, pulling it off the stick. The white goo oozed out along the rim with some chocolate. She held it to his lips. "Here you go."

He took a bite of the sticky concoction, he'd forgotten how much he loved s'mores. Even more, he loved watching her assemble her own snack. When a dribble of marshmallow lingered at the corner of her mouth, he almost had to sit on his hands to stop himself from reaching over and wiping it off. Or worse, kissing away the sweet dollop.

Whatever was he thinking? This is Kyle's little sister. In his mind, he'd begun doing some fast math. She'd mentioned finishing school, traveling, working on her photography, odd jobs and career plans, and just like that it hit him that Kyle Baron's little sister was actually at least a year or two older than Connie. And didn't that put a whole new perspective on his best friend's little sister?

The way Jack was attacking the s'more, anyone would think he'd never had one before. The oddest part of it was, rather than be annoyed, Siobhan was loving watching the way his eyes danced with delight at every bite.

"Had your fill?" Jack stabbed a stick with another marshmallow.

Swallowing the lick of embarrassment that had crept up at being caught staring at him, she was pretty sure he was referring to the marshmallows and not him. *Maybe.* "Just getting started." She smiled back at him before mimicking his motions and shoving two marshmallows onto her stick.

"A challenge?" he teased.

That grin was killing her. How had she never noticed growing up what a great smile the man had? And those eyes? How had her sister not found them irresistible? A couple of times she thought she'd caught him staring at her with a spark of longing that had made her insides go warm and her mouth go dry. Then, just as quickly, the look had slipped away and she told herself she'd been imagining things.

"You missed a dollop." Jack's hands reached out and the tip of his finger swiped away a dribble of marshmallow from the corner of her mouth. The momentary warmth of his fingertip had her insides melting faster than the marshmallows. It took everything in her not to close her eyes and lean into his touch. What was going on here? Jack was like another big brother. And more than a few years older than her, she was sure her friends would think she'd lost her mind. Heck, only a few weeks ago she'd teased Mitch that he was turning into an old man and now here she was simmering under the gaze of her older brother's dearest friend. Maybe she *had* gone nuts?

A deep frown replaced Jack's sweet and sexy grin. "Is something wrong? Did you burn yourself?" His hand reached for her hand and she quickly pulled it away.

The last thing she needed right now was for him to

touch her. "Just remembering I have an early appointment tomorrow."

"Oh." The worry disappeared from his face, but the twinkle hadn't returned to his eyes. "It's been a long day, we should call it a night."

She shook her head. "I didn't mean we had to leave now. I was just…thinking."

"No." He set up one last s'more and held it up. "I'll finish this and tell John it's been a great party but I have to leave."

Now she was mad at herself. She didn't want tonight to end. She could not for the life of her remember the last time she'd had such a perfect day—and evening. But he was probably right. Going home was the smart thing to do. The prudent thing to do. Disappear before Jack Preston got too deeply under her skin. Then again, when had anyone ever called her prudent?

Taking her dear sweet time to slowly nibble on her last double marshmallow s'more, she popped the last morsel in her mouth and begrudgingly pushed to her feet when Jack stood and extended his hand for her.

The spark of electricity that zipped up her arm actually had her looking around to see if anyone had seen what she felt. From the quick way that Jack had let go, she'd have sworn he'd felt it too. Or maybe that was just her wishful thinking again. Heaving out a sigh, she followed in his footsteps, thanking people as they passed, wishing the birthday boy a successful and happy year one last time before they climbed into his car.

"Thanks for tagging along." He hit the ignition switch and flashed her a smile that didn't quite reach his eyes. "I'm beat and it really helped having a good reason to call it an early night."

"Are you sure you wanted to leave?" She really did feel awful pulling him away from his friends.

"Positive. You've worn these old bones out."

And there it was in front of her. Jack Preston was indeed older than her. Not crazy old, like he could be her father or anything icky like that. But old enough to have grown up in two different decades and should have nothing in common. And yet, she'd had such an easy time talking to him about everything and anything for the last couple of days.

Damn. Why did the nicest guy she'd met in forever have to be her brother's best friend?

The drive home had proven shorter than she would have liked. The SUV pulled into the Paradise Ridge driveway and came to a stop at the front doors. It probably would be considered childish if she pouted and refused to get out of the car. In the time she'd chastised herself for thinking like a kid, Jack had circled the hood and opened her door.

She noticed that unlike before, he didn't hold his hand out for her. Could it be she'd been right? He had felt the zap of electricity the way she had. Arguing with herself, she made her way up the stairs, fidgeting in her bag for the keys. She yanked them out and spun around to thank Jack for a lovely day. Only to her surprise he wasn't just on the porch, he was directly behind her. So close that as she spun, she bumped into him, forcing him to grab both her arms to steady her. "Sorry!"

"No. I shouldn't have been so close."

His gaze seemed to burn into her. And why was he still holding her arms? Her heartbeat kicked into double time and she found herself rolling forward on her feet. She could feel the heat of his gaze all the way to her soul. This she was not by any means imagining.

"Siobhan." Her name on his lips came out low, sweet, and sounded almost like a prayer. He leaned forward and her breath caught. He was going to kiss her. Inching up on her tippy toes, the anticipation had her heart racing and her hopes soaring.

Their faces were so close she could feel the warmth of his breath caressing her lips. Just another few inches and she'd be in heaven.

"Long day?" The front door swung open.

The two of them sprang apart like a couple of teens caught necking on the family sofa.

"Very." Jack turned to face her brother Mitch, taking a

step in retreat at the same time. "I've got a longer one tomorrow, need to get going." He turned to face her while taking yet another step back. "Thanks again for helping with Mom's gift, and for today."

Her head bobbed but the words "You're welcome" were stuck in her throat. Another few seconds and his taillights were disappearing in the distance.

"You coming in or planning on staying on the porch all night?" Her brother's tone was less than pleasant.

What she really wanted to do was run after the car and…and what? The litany of possibilities that ran through her mind had her shaking her head. Boy, was she in trouble.

CHAPTER NINE

Despite not seeing her for a week, Jack couldn't get Siobhan out of his mind. Even at work, bogged down with deadlines and demands, and every time he had a moment to himself, visions of Siobhan laughing and singing in the front seat of his car made him smile. Technically, the kid was now a grown woman. She was also his best friend's little sister. More than a few years younger than him, and no matter how smart and fun and fascinating he found her—she was still off limits according to the Bro Code.

Why couldn't she be related to perfect strangers? Or any other family on the planet would work. Just not the Barons. The most interesting woman he'd spent time with in years and thanks to genetics and a sense of honor—she was off-limits.

Staring at the freezer section of the grocery store, he contemplated which microwave meals held the most appeal. None of the boxes inspired him, but he had to eat. What he wanted was to call Siobhan and invite her for dinner. Which itself wasn't much of a problem. The wanting to keep her at his side till breakfast was more of the sticking point. None of the four Baron brothers, nor the litany of cousins, would take kindly to that idea. He'd come home from work too late and too tired to boil water, never mind actually cook. And like old Mother Hubbard, his cupboards, or more precisely his fridge, was bare.

Who the heck ever came up with the Bro Code anyway? He snagged the first five boxes of frozen dinners he saw on the freezer shelf. After all, shouldn't a brother be thrilled that a friend they knew and trusted was interested—okay, more than interested—in their sister? Of course, knowing exactly how many oats he'd sown and with whom was probably not the best letter of recommendation. Shaking off thoughts of Siobhan, and her brothers tearing him limb from limb if he laid a finger on her, he momentarily studied his cart and dinners for the next few days. He was also out of toothpaste. That would be one aisle over.

Smiling at the woman pushing a cart with a little kid happily gurgling in the seat, he wondered when had he started noticing women and their children. Another thing he could credit Siobhan for. The woman looked so gorgeous holding a baby. He could almost picture her surrounded by little girls who looked just like her and little boys who looked like him. This was insane. He had to get Siobhan out of his head. Somehow. Halfway up the aisle, his feet and heart stuttered to a stop. Was he hallucinating now?

Nope. Turning into the aisle was the one and only Siobhan Baron. He debated backing out of the aisle. How many people would he trample escaping the woman he couldn't get out of his mind? Time apart hadn't done a thing to dampen his attraction for her. If anything, it was getting worse. Maybe he should just leave the cart and order pizza for dinner. That would be the only way to escape the aisle without her spotting him.

Did that make him a coward? What if she recognized him running away? What would she think? Blast. When had Siobhan become such a complication for him? Oh yeah, the minute she'd smiled at him.

"Jack?"

The decision to stand his ground or run had been made for him.

"Hi. This is a surprise." Was his voice neutral enough? It sounded a bit squeaky to him. Like he'd been caught with his hands in the cookie jar.

"A good one, I hope?" The obvious delight, blended with a hint of teasing in her voice, made his heart skip a beat.

"Absolutely." And he meant it; Bro Code or not, she'd just become the highlight of his day, even if only for a few minutes in the grocery aisle. "This isn't your part of town."

"No, popped in for a bottle of Gatorade and a bag of chips. I'm shooting some new photos. Something different for that gallery I told you about. I finally got a chance to chat with Veronica, the owner. She seemed to genuinely like my work, but implied even with professional recognition, like a ribbon from the State Fair, some diversity might be needed. I've been focused on recognition, but figured I should probably work on finding something different, so I've abandoned wildlife for a day in the city."

"I'm guessing that doesn't include the toothpaste aisle of my local supermarket."

That smile sucker punched him. "Not quite." Eyes sparkling with humor were driving him crazy. "Doing a little experimenting with the local architecture." She eyed his cart. "Frozen dinners and toothpaste. Interesting combination."

"Stick around. I need shampoo too."

That had her laughing out loud and him wondering how awful would it be to spend just a little more time with her.

"You should try cooking. I doubt that frozen lasagna tastes much better than cardboard."

"Cooking and I are not the best of friends. Mom tried to teach me but it pretty much went over like a lead balloon. Though I do grill a mean steak."

"I love cooking. At my flat in Ireland, I experiment with all sorts of recipes, but not so much here in the States with Hazel at the ranch doing all the cooking."

Her own flat in Ireland? Of course she could have her own apartment. He had his own condo. He had to remind himself, little sister or not, she was no longer a kid but a grown woman—and that was the crux of his problem. "What do you cook?"

Wrinkling her nose in the direction of his cart, she waved a finger at it. "For one thing, my lasagna would taste way better than that cardboard box you have there."

"You make lasagna?"

"Better than an Italian." Her chin high and shoulders

back, she beamed up at him. "Someday, I'll make it for you. You'll see."

"How about tonight?"

"Tonight?" Her eyes widened.

"Unless you have other plans, we'll pick up the ingredients and you can come to my place and do all the cooking you want."

Siobhan cocked her head. And for a moment he thought he'd really stuck his foot in it. Been too forward. Considered that perhaps his interest in her was a one-way street. Relief flooded through him when that same smile spread across her face. "Okay. Deal."

"But I'll be buying the ingredients."

"You don't—"

She didn't have to say a word, the narrowed glare she tossed in his direction silenced him faster than had she covered his mouth with a gag.

"Thank you."

"I'll make two trays this way you'll have some leftovers."

Whatever she said after that was going in one ear and out the other. With every item she grabbed from the shelf, the enthusiasm in her voice lifted. Whether it was over spending time with him or having an opportunity to cook, he didn't know and didn't care. The bottom line was tonight he wouldn't have to conjure her memory up in his mind, he was going to soak in every face-to-face minute. Tomorrow he'd worry about tomorrow. And the Barons. And if he was going to live to see the day after.

The kitchen in Jack's condo was to die for. Walls of white flat-front cabinets filled the large space. If the amazing amount of cabinets wasn't enough to impress her, she stirred her sauce and drank in the top-shelf appliances. She couldn't get over-the-counter space either. Oh, the fun she would have creating meals in this kitchen.

Seated at the massive granite-covered island, a glass of Zinfandel in front of him, Jack watched her every move as if he would need to pass a test on it shortly. "How long does the lasagna take?"

"Normally, I would make the sauce from scratch, but that takes a few hours. Since I'm pretty sure you don't want dinner at midnight, I'm cheating, simmering jarred sauce for about thirty minutes with the sautéed beef while the noodles cook. In the meantime, I'm going to add some sausage too for a little more flavor. Then it will just be a matter of putting the lasagna together and another twenty minutes or so in the oven."

"We have all night."

For food, she shouted silently, forcing herself not to read into that statement. Jack was being nice. Probably craving a home-cooked meal. Spending more time with her most likely had nothing to do with tonight's cooking show. "I bet you're pretty hungry."

"Actually, watching you, I'm famished."

And didn't that send her mind to inappropriate places. "For a man who doesn't cook, you sure have a stocked state-of-the-art kitchen. I've never seen so many baking pans in one place."

He smiled back at her. "We aim to please."

Once again, her mind was ready and willing to let her imagination run wild. If she didn't get it under wraps, and fast, this was going to be a very long night.

"Anything I can do to help?" He pushed away from the island and stood.

"You want to brown the sausage?" She waved a spoon at the empty frying pan. As much as she liked watching the way the corded muscles of his neck moved with every sip of wine, or how the fabric of his t-shirt pulled against hard biceps every time he raised his glass to his lips, the prospect of the two of them standing side by side held a great deal more appeal.

"Absolutely. Sausage in a frying pan is a lot like breakfast. I can do breakfast."

She refused to let her mind wander to how many times

he must have made breakfast for two. Instead, she reached forward and turned on the burner.

Jack pierced the sausage with a fork and tossed the links into the pan. He rolled and flipped each one with practiced ease. *Yep.* Lots of breakfasts.

"Am I doing this right?" The warmth of his arm bumped against her as she stirred the noodles in the massive pot beside the frying pan.

Of all people to have a single touch light her up from the inside out, why did it have to be Jack? So many reasons this man was so off-limits. Facing down her brothers was at the top of the list. "Hard to mess up sausage."

"Cooked enough to add to the sauce?"

She bobbed her head. That came easier at the moment than making polite chit-chat while his arm was still pressed against hers.

Stabbing the first link with the fork, he dropped it into the pot. The second link refused to slide off the prongs. Jack used his finger to gently shove it forward. "Ow."

"Careful." She let go of her spoon, wiped her hands on a dishrag. Jack stuck his finger in his mouth and Siobhan almost swallowed her tongue as his cheeks moved with the motions of sucking at the pained finger. Getting a grip of her runaway imagination, she reached for his hand. "Let me see."

"It's nothing."

"Those sausages are covered in hot grease. It can burn you more than you think."

Gently she turned the fingertip, looking for any sign of blistering. She didn't dare look up, but she was sure his gaze was burning a hole through her. "Let's run it under cold water."

"It's fine." He made no effort to retrieve his hand or move toward the sink.

She could be stubborn. Hands on her hips, she didn't budge until he did as he was told and ran the red finger under cold water. The burn taken care of, they resumed the cooking process. Somehow she made it through all the casual touches as he helped her layer the casserole, and through the lingering glances and heartfelt chuckles as he told stories of his escapades with her brother, including having the teachers catch them in a girl's room—innocently, according to him—during an outing to New York City in high school. She'd almost peed her pants from laughing while the lasagna baked.

Looking around the well-appointed condo, for a single man, the place was huge. Her little flat in Dublin could fit in the living and dining room alone. "Did you decorate this yourself?"

"If I had, it would have nothing but sports posters and theater seating." Jack chuckled. "Though I did set up my office on my own. The decorator wanted to give me this rather stuffy man cave but I needed practical."

"Do you work from home?"

"Sometimes. A lot of time I have to be in the office, but some days I can get as much done from home, especially if I don't have to waste time commuting."

"Are you still making people rich trading in the financial markets?"

His brows shot up. "How did you know that?"

"Is it a secret?"

"Well, no." He shrugged.

"I have excellent hearing, a near-perfect memory, and you and my brothers talked markets and investments as often as you talked sports, racing and girls."

"Oh." His gaze dropped to the silverware on the table and she was pretty sure he actually blushed at her voicing out loud her knowledge of her brother and his escapades with the female of the species. "Yes, I'm still in finance."

The buzzer on the oven sounded and she pulled the lasagna out and carried it over to the trivet on the table. A few moments more and their dinner was served. Seated across the table from him, she couldn't decide if she was disappointed or grateful for the distance.

Lifting her wine glass, she touched it to his. "To lasagna."

His glass clinked against hers. "To chance encounters."

Yes, she thought. Thank heaven for the fates.

"This is amazing." Jack gazed up at her as strings of mozzarella dangled from his fork. "Even Hazel's lasagna can't beat this. I can't imagine the long version."

"I'll have to make it for you some day when there's more time."

"I'd like that." His smile softened, his fork stilled and his gaze tore through her like a heated bolt of lightening.

"Thank you." Breaking the hold his gaze had on her, she looked down at her fork, carefully stabbing at a morsel of dinner. "I noticed a park around the corner. I think I've got some nice contrast shots with the city photos – but the park struck me as having lots of possibilities for capturing something more. Tomorrow I was thinking of going there and taking a few photos." She dared to meet his gaze again. "Care to join me?"

"I'd love to."

The smile that took over her face matched the bright grin Jack flashed at her. She had no idea why she'd invited him. Until she'd opened her mouth, she hadn't even remembered the park or thought of taking pictures. Now she needed every ounce of decorum she possessed not to jump to her feet and hug him, beyond delighted that he wanted to spend more time with her. Not eat her cooking, not help out the baby sister of the family, but just be with her. How cool was that?

CHAPTER TEN

"**S**quirrel!" Jack's head snapped to the right, his arm pointing in the same direction.

"You sound like that dog from the kid's movie." Siobhan didn't try to hide her amusement at Jack's antics.

Lifting his hands in the air, he flashed a toothy grin and shrugged. "You said you wanted squirrels."

"I did." On her belly, camera pointed in the direction Jack had pointed, Siobhan took a picture of a squirrel who'd become curious, holding a nut in his front claws, the little guy—or gal—inched closer and closer to her, stopping only yards away. She snapped away until the sound of the shutter drove the squirrel to run to the nearest tree for safety. "That one was close."

"I don't know that I've ever seen such a curious squirrel." Jack had sat on the grass only a foot or so away from her. "If you feed them, I bet even more would dare to come closer."

Siobhan shook her head. "That's cheating. I like to get the ones who will come closer on their own. Those have the most personality and will do more interesting things. Sometimes."

"If you say so." Humor laced his words.

Only now did she realize that he'd remained frozen to allow her the close-up shot before speaking. Considering she'd dragged him out here on a lark, with no plans in mind, he was being a good sport about just hanging with her as she searched out the more interesting photos of city wildlife.

Houston was a big place. Though she was familiar with

the surrounding up-and-coming areas in general, this was the first time she'd stumbled across this particular park. She rather liked it. Heavy with woods on one side and a somewhat forgotten playground on the other, in between the park sported a large swath of grass with enough space for kids to play soccer, adults and their dogs to play Frisbee or fetch, and plenty of room to spare.

On her elbows, Siobhan eased herself up, spotting a woman sitting on a mat with her legs crossed, her eyes closed. Rolled-up mats perched beside her in a pyramid.

"Ooh, look."

Jack's gaze narrowed as he looked off in the distance. Shaking his head, he turned to her. "More squirrels?"

"Yoga."

"Yoga?"

"Yep." She packed away her camera and then smiled up at him. "We should join them. It'll be fun."

"Fun?" He chuckled lightly. "For an old lady maybe."

"Old lady?" She glared at him. "Yoga has excellent health benefits. Lowers stress, builds core strength, keeps you limber."

"I have plenty of core strength, am limber enough—when it counts—and I like my stress, thank you."

She felt heat rush up her cheeks at his little innuendo and literally shook her thoughts away. "Oh, come on. Give it a try."

He shook his head. "Can't. Didn't bring any cash with me."

"Hmm." She watched the woman work the other attendees through some breathing exercises. "First class is often free. We should ask."

He eyed the scene with skepticism, then shook his head again. "Nope. I can make a fool of myself some other way."

"Okay." She plopped herself on the grass again, tugging at the hem of Jack's shirt. "Let's just follow the class from here."

Jack's gaze darted left then right, over to the woman now on all fours. "I don't know."

"Chicken?"

He rolled his eyes. "Five minutes. That's all you get."

"Deal." She waited for him to sit beside her, then she crawled onto all fours like the instructor across the lawn was doing.

"This is easy enough." Jack smiled.

"She hasn't really started yet."

His brows inched up his forehead. "Could have fooled me."

The woman's one leg went up in the air behind her. "Now she's starting."

Siobhan did the same, casting a sideways glance at Jack doing the same, only a lot more wobbly than anyone else. The woman changed to the other leg. "And change."

"This is silly." Jack shifted sides, raising his other leg and almost toppling over. "Really silly."

"You need to work on your balance."

"My balance is just fine on two legs. If men were meant to be down on all fours, the good Lord would have given us four legs and no arms."

On her hands, the instructor inched her hands closer to the middle of the mat, slowly raising her bum straight in the air.

"Now that's easy. Silly, but easy." Jack moved to the downward facing dog position in one move.

"Straighten your back. You're not supposed to have your back arched in the downward dog."

"Downward dog?" Tilting his head, he faced her. "Who the heck named it that?"

She shrugged and moved over to place her hand on his back. "I have no idea who named it, but you need to straighten your back. It's that core thing."

Her hand on his back, he groaned and then one hand slipped out from under him. Next thing she knew, he was flat on the ground and she was sprawled over him. How he'd taken her out so easily, she had no idea. The whole endeavor went from bad to worse.

He'd managed to do okay with the warrior pose but when they shifted to the triangle, once again he toppled over, taking her with him. "Are you sure it wouldn't be easier to play Twister? At least then we're supposed to keep falling over."

"Twister doesn't relieve stress."

"Neither does this." His chuckle eased into a real laugh.

As soon as the instructor shifted to the half-moon pose, Siobhan knew they were in trouble. She'd started, trying to casually spy on him beside her. For a few seconds they both balanced perfectly, despite the giggles. "See, you got this."

"What I have is a cramp in my leg." He brought his leg down to the ground and turned to face her at the same moment she twisted to see the instructor.

Instead of finding the teacher, she found Jack up close and beside her. The shock of it had her tumbling over, knocking Jack off his legs until he landed splat on top of her.

The two of them cracked up laughing until she realized his breath was warm against her, and his face was so close she could see the gray flecks in his deep blue eyes. She almost lost her breath and softly muttered, "Sorry."

"No. My fault." He didn't move, only inched himself up so she could breathe. Maybe. "Siobhan?"

"Mm hm?"

He didn't say a word, just dipped a fraction closer until his lips covered hers.

Oh, damn. Her arms wrapped around him as she kissed him back. Something in the back of her head said this was all wrong, but another part knew it was very right.

In his time Jack had kissed many women, but kissing Siobhan today sent a bevy of feelings and emotions surging through him that he'd never felt from a simple, sweet kiss before in his life. When he found himself close enough to feel the race of her heartbeat against his, and her face so close he could feel her breathe, at that moment, she wasn't anyone's sister, she wasn't too young, and she wasn't off limits. Not even a hurricane could have stopped him from doing what he'd been avoiding for days.

Even now, back in the car and on the way home, his lips still tingled long after the loss of her touch. It had taken every bit of common sense and willpower to pull back. For the life of him, he couldn't tell if she was shocked, scared, pleased, or as overwhelmed by the kiss as he'd been. Wide-eyed, she'd barely blinked, simply stared at him. Never had he known anyone who looked so darn enticing, just lying on the grass, leveling her gaze with his.

When he'd come up for air, she hadn't said a word or tried to scramble away. He hadn't a clue what to do or say, the only words he could find were, "We should get going." Still looking at him, she merely nodded and sat up. He hadn't dared reach for her to help her up for fear he'd wind up right back where he'd started, on the ground, up close and personal, wanting so much more than he should.

It had taken a short while for either of them to find their voice. They'd walked to the car in total silence. He'd considered apologizing, but didn't want to. If he could, he'd do it again. A lot. As soon as he'd turned the radio on, she seemed to snap back to herself. A bright smile took over her face at some song he hadn't recognized, and when she turned to him, grinning and bopping in her seat again, his heart soared and he smiled back.

Just like that, they seemed to be on an even keel. What he didn't know was what to do next. Like it or not, she had four big brothers who he knew beyond any doubt were not going to cotton to his crushing on their sister.

Another song came on and she danced in her seat once again, singing at the top of her lungs. Singing so loud that the cars at the light beside them could probably hear her through the closed windows. Anyone else and he would have suggested they take a break before they caused a scene, but with Siobhan, he merely wanted to roll down the windows and shout to the world—this is my girl.

My girl. Was that what he wanted? Because if it wasn't, he'd better walk—no, run—the other way. This was not someone to be toyed with—regardless of who her brothers were. Siobhan was the kind of woman who deserved a man ready and able to make a commitment. A word he'd never before considered. Could he be that man? What to do next, what to say, had been kicking around in his mind when the traffic ahead slowed.

"This is odd for a Saturday afternoon?"

"This is Houston. Traffic is a way of life."

"I know, but not like this. We're almost at a stop." She stopped her dancing and sat up straighter in her seat, trying to see what was ahead.

"Probably construction. The city likes nothing better than tearing up the streets and making the drivers crazy."

"I hope that's it."

Barely inching along, he glanced in her direction. Focused on the road ahead, it almost seemed as if kissing her was an ordinary, everyday thing. What a great idea. Kiss Siobhan every day.

"Oh, no." Her gaze narrowed as the cars blended into a single lane to avoid the debris on the side of the road leading up to the police and fire trucks ahead. "It's an accident. This many first responders can't be a good sign."

Two crumpled cars sat on the side of the road, one straight ahead with its front end missing, the other at an awkward angle with the trunk pretty much in the backseat. An ambulance's back door was wide open and he could barely see two EMTs in their white shirts working over a gurney. He could only assume they were helping a victim.

"Someone's been hurt." Siobhan gnawed on her lower lip when the sound of a siren had them both looking up. Another ambulance was making its way through the bottleneck of cars. "Oh, no."

He glanced around, looking for more victims when he noticed Siobhan bow her head. Her lips moved in silence. She was praying. Texas was the buckle of the bible belt. Finding someone who believed in the power of God was nothing unusual, and yet, seeing her living her faith, concerned for people she didn't know, struck him harder than any blow her brothers could give.

Merged into the single lane, they drove past the frenzy of police and firemen as the first ambulance sped away, lights flashing and sirens blaring. He found himself raising his gaze to the sky and asking God to guide the hands of the rescuers and perform a miracle. How many years had it been since he remembered there even was a god?

Something inside Jack shifted at the sight of Siobhan praying. They picked up speed and left the accident behind them. The seriousness of what was going on between them came front and center. He wasn't sure of much right now, but he was sure of one thing, he would guard her heart like his own. He did not want to lose Siobhan in his life—if she would have him. All he had to figure out was what to do now.

CHAPTER ELEVEN

Several photos from the park shoot the other day were strewn across Siobhan's workroom. She was hoping to have enough to stop by and show Veronica that she'd taken her advice about diversity to heart, but nothing had struck her as just right on her computer screen. In hopes that something would pop, she'd gone ahead and printed the best. Studying them carefully, she frowned—no such luck.

At least she didn't think so. Her normally critical eye and sharp instincts eluded her. The only thing she seemed to be able to fully focus on was that kiss. Jack Preston had kissed her. Not a *Kyle's kid sister* peck on the cheek. A real, honest-to-goodness, toe curling, mouth on mouth kiss, and no matter how she tried to dive in to work the last few days, her mind kept revisiting the surreal moment.

Her lips still remembered the feel of his. She found herself resting her fingertips on her lips, the feel of his touch still lingered. If she closed her eyes, she could relive the moment over and over. And how stupid would that look? Wouldn't she have a fun time explaining that to her family if any had walked in on her and noticed? Pleading the fifth wouldn't cut it. Maybe she could claim she was coming down with something. Heaven knows, a fever would certainly be a more acceptable explanation for her behavior than confessing that the mere thought of Jack made her feel warm over.

Of course that left her with a new conundrum. Why hadn't he called her? Was he embarrassed? Did he regret kissing her? She really hoped it wasn't the latter, because she most definitely wanted him to do it again. Maybe she should call him? After all, this was the age of equality. A girl could call a boy. Except she didn't have a clue what to say; Can we roll around on the grass and kiss some more didn't seem quite right—though true.

"Those photos are lovely." Grams stood in Siobhan's doorway.

"Thanks." Startled out of her ruminations over Jack, she returned her attention to the photographs staring blankly at her. "I'm just not sure I like them enough to show them to Veronica at the gallery or even bother entering at the State Fair."

"They are good." Her grandmother stepped into the room. "But you want something better."

"Yes, exactly."

"Perhaps," her grandmother smiled at the photos before turning to face her, "you might consider something with more of a statement?"

That made Siobhan frown in thought. Statement? Her mind ran to grittier, darker, meaningful. At the park where she'd taken the photos of the curious squirrels, there'd been a playground. A bit run down, but still in use. Yes. Siobhan nodded, deciding at the moment to hurry out. "I've got an idea. I won't be home too late. I need to take a few more shots and add them to the portfolio before my meeting tomorrow afternoon."

Placing a hand on her shoulder, Lila Conroe Baron smiled at her. "It's the Baron way. We're never satisfied with mediocre."

Tucked away at one end of the park, the forlorn playground stood empty. Already she could picture the shots she wanted. Hopefully, these would do the trick. She set her camera bags on a nearby bench while she considered the light, the equipment, and what she hoped to achieve. A woman with a dog on a leash and a little girl in a stroller walked by the perimeter of the playground. The little girl stretched her arm over the side of the stroller, calling for her mom to stop.

"Five minutes," the woman told the little girl.

Siobhan watched as the child climbed onto the rocking hippo that had seen better days, then scurried over to one of those old-fashioned carousels. The kind that had been removed from most playgrounds in more upscale neighborhoods. The little girl grabbed onto the handle and ran around making it spin, giggling like, well, a happy little girl. Siobhan couldn't resist and snapped a photo, one after the other. She'd have to get a release if she intended to use these for professional purposes. As the mother notified the child that she had one minute left, Siobhan ran up to her and handed the mom a business card. At the end of the minute, she had the woman's name and phone number to contact in the event she did indeed choose one of these photos for the show. That is, if Veronica agreed.

The playground empty again, Siobhan began clicking away at the paint chipped monkey bars, imagining the day when the equipment was shiny and new and most likely crawling with neighborhood children. Over her shoulder she heard voices and glanced behind her. Two young men in jeans and ball caps were walking in her direction from the parking lot. A little old for the playground was the first thing to cross her mind. The next thought she reminded herself, whatever they were up to was none of her business.

Returning to her camera lens, one of the guys muttered a hello, and she barely dared to nod at them. A moment later they took seats on a bench across from where she was. They could have chosen ten other benches. Why did they need to be by her? The hairs on the back of her neck rising, she gathered her equipment and moved to the other side of the playground. The light would be more challenging, but at least she'd put some distance between herself and the two guys.

A few mediocre photos later, another muttered word she couldn't quite make out and she realized the men were seated across from her again. What flustered her more than their presence was that they were perfectly planted between her and the exit route to her car.

Using her lens to examine her exit routes without drawing suspicion, something in her gut told her she really should have brought someone with her. Letting her camera dangle around her neck, she pulled out her phone to call…who? Speed dialing the Governor, the call went straight to voicemail. The men stood and moved one bench closer. She didn't like that one bit. Tapping hard at her keyboard, she called the one person she knew she could trust as much as her own kin. Jack.

Feeling like a heroine in a cheap horror flick who was too stupid to save herself, she linked her arm through the camera bag strap, ready to wield it like a weapon. On the other end, the phone rang once, twice, and she looked away from the men. No one else in view, her car so far out of the way, her palms beginning to sweat. "Come on, Jack."

That kiss. Jack wished he could stop thinking about Siobhan and that mind-blowing kiss. If he somehow managed to push away the memory of how her lips felt against his, then other visions of Siobhan crept into his head. The way she smiled when she held a baby, the way her voice softened and her eyes sparkled when she talked on the phone to her mama, the way she willingly jumps in where needed, whether helping a mom with a stroller or saying a silent prayer. All of it made his insides go soft and his heart want to dance.

Everything new he learned about her continued to highlight just how special she was. Not that it mattered. Days had gone by and he hadn't called her. Instead, he'd dunked himself in work. Those same Irish eyes that drove him crazy with light and laughter were probably spewing daggers at the thought of him. Who kissed a girl then went silent? And his best friend's sister, no less. There was no excuse for crossing the line and kissing her, never mind going silent afterward. He was behaving like a teenager.

What he needed to do was make time to talk to her brothers. There would be no going forward without declaring his intentions to them first. Of course, that required he knew what his intentions were and right now, he couldn't be more confused if he really were still a teenager.

Tonight. At the benefit. Normally, a public gathering was not the ideal place for this type of conversation, but the risk of one or all of her siblings killing him in front of witnesses was greatly decreased.

On his desk at his side, his phone buzzed, pulling him out of his thoughts. Siobhan's name came onto his screen, making him smile. Maybe she wasn't mad at him after all. "Hello."

"Jack. I need your help."

The desperation in her voice grabbed him by the throat and propelled him to the edge of his seat. "Always. What's wrong?"

"I'm back at the playground near the park not far from your place. There are some men here and they are making me nervous."

Phone to his ear, he'd already grabbed his keys and was halfway to the front door. "I know where you are. Put me on hold and call 911."

"But they haven't done anything, I mean, besides creep me out."

"Trust your instincts. Can you get to your car?"

"No, that's the problem. They keep shifting to stay in between me and the parking lot."

"Hold tight. I'm getting into my car now. Be there in five minutes." A sense of panic raced up Jack's spine. A simple visit to the park could easily turn into tonight's six o'clock news headline. He didn't like it one bit. "Don't hang up."

"I won't." Her voice sounded so small, so unlike the bright vivacious woman he'd gotten to know over the last week. "Jack?"

Silently, he cussed at the last red light between him and the park. "Yes?"

"I'm scared." She spoke so softly, he almost couldn't hear her.

"I'm almost there. It will be fine." It has to be. Suddenly, he knew exactly what his intentions toward Siobhan were; everything he'd ever avoided, commitment, home, hearth, and lots of children with her fiery red hair and bright smile.

His heart slammed a rapid beat against his ribs. Blasted Houston traffic. He needed to get to Siobhan—now.

The minutes ticked away as Jack kept her talking. Asking why she was at the park? Had she gotten any good pictures? She answered each question as he ignored the speed limit and took the turn into the parking lot on two wheels. Shoving the car in park, he had the door open and bolted toward the playground, desperately searching for her.

A sigh of relief struck when he spotted her on a bench, still talking to him, followed by a rush of adrenaline as the two men in question seemed to be closing in on her.

"Hey, honey. Sorry I'm late." He waved his arm and eased his pace to a slow gallop.

She smiled his way. The fear in Siobhan's eyes scraped his heart into pieces. He touched her arm and relief sprung into those beautiful eyes.

The two men froze in place and turned to look him up and down. At least, if this was about to get messy, he had size on his side. And a few pounds.

Choosing to pretend he wasn't here to rescue his damsel in distress, he reached for her hand and pulled her to her feet, planting another all too brief kiss on her lips. As much as he wanted to keep her pressed against him, he needed to keep an eye on the reason he was here. To his relief, both men took a few steps in retreat. Jack's fingers skipped down her arm and grabbing her hand, laced their fingers together, ready to make a run for it if needed.

"I want to go home." She kept her eyes leveled with his. "Can we get out of here?"

"Absolutely. Stick with me."

She nodded, and he surveyed their surroundings. The two guys had fallen back to the park periphery and away from them. "Thanks, Jack. I appreciate you coming to the rescue for what was probably nothing."

"Know that you can always count on me." Taking another moment to watch the two men walking away toward a crop of trees, somehow, Jack had no doubt those two were up to no good. He didn't even want to consider what could have happened to Siobhan if he hadn't been working from home today.

"Just what I needed." She forced a stronger smile. "Another big brother."

"Not at all." He closed her small fist in his. "You got any plans tonight?"

She sighed. "Whole family is going to Mitch's fundraiser."

"Come with me?"

"With you?"

He nodded. "Be my date?"

"Date?"

Again, he nodded, trying not to feel horribly insecure at her hesitant reaction. "I promise to behave."

That elicited the deep laugh he was hoping for. "Not so sure that's a good thing, but yes. I'd be happy to be your date. Only, I have a bunch of things to take care of, is it okay if I meet you there?"

"Whatever the lady wants." As much as it went against his mother's upbringing to not pick a date up at her door, having a bit of time to speak with her siblings would be a good thing. Or, if things went south, at least she wouldn't have to witness her brothers committing murder.

CHAPTER TWELVE

The first stop after the park for Siobhan was the gallery. Overflowing with trendy cafes, boutiques, and new-age stores, the ever-growing arts section of Houston was on her way home. It had been a spur-of-the-moment decision, fueled by her excitement over today's photos and tonight's prospects; she simply couldn't wait to show Veronica. Loaded with a stack of photos and what was on her camera, she pushed the front door open.

The dinging of the front door brought the gallery owner out from her office in the back. "Siobhan, so good to see you."

"Glad you were available to see me on short notice. I'm excited about a few pictures."

Siobhan laid out the ones she'd printed on a table in the office. The woman mulled over them, nodding and sighing and pressing her lips together, she looked up at Siobhan. "What else?"

Now she wished she'd waited to call Veronica until after she'd printed the photos from the park. Pulling out her camera, she scrolled to today's shoot and handed it over to Veronica.

A little brighter with each swipe through what Siobhan had taken that day, a slow smile hovered on the woman's face. "I love these."

Siobhan let out a relieved sigh. "Thank you."

"I have a Belgian artist scheduled for a one-woman show in three weeks. She's had some trouble with her visas. We're going to have to cancel." Veronica strolled around her desk and flipped through a calendar. Her finger still on the page, she lifted her gaze to meet Siobhan's. "Want her spot?"

"Excuse me?" Siobhan struggled for another coherent thought.

Veronica chuckled. "Don't look so surprised. These are good. Very good. The stark contrast of Houston's neighborhoods was a brilliant idea. Between the two of us, we can determine the best of your portfolio. With a little hard work, I think we can just about make the deadline for your own show. Are you in?"

"Absolutely." Her head bobbed so fast, she wouldn't have been surprised if it snapped off her shoulders. A smile tugged at the corners of her mouth and she couldn't help but wonder if today could possibly get any better.

Next thing she knew, Siobhan was signing contracts, talking size of prints, framing, deadlines, agreeing on a next meeting to finalize the prints to use, and finally shaking hands before heading out the door and hurrying home. Siobhan would move heaven and earth to get the pictures done in time, and could hardly wait to see Jack and tell him in person.

Jack. The man who hadn't hesitated when she'd called for his help. The man who had kissed her as if his—or her—life depended on it. How had he become so important to her in such a short amount of time? She sighed as she surveyed her closet for what to wear. The invitation hadn't been completely clear. Whether she was to be his new just-for-show plus one the way Eve had been for so many years, or a real honest-to-goodness date, she had no idea.

What she did know was that more than anything she wanted the latter—after all, he had kissed her. Surely that wasn't a boring plus one kiss. Most definitely, she wanted Jack to sit up and take notice that she was very much grown up and very much interested in more than friends. Reaching into her closet, she pulled out a green dress and a pair of green strappy sandals to finish off the outfit. This was the dress that garnered her the most compliments.

Her grandmother poked her head into her room. "Your grandfather and I are heading out early to help Mitch greet his guests. Since you don't look ready, shall I send the driver back to get you?"

And Jack would drive her home. That thought made her smile. "That would be fantastic, Grams. I should be ready by then."

Her grandmother nodded, eyeing the dress Siobhan had laid out. "Good choice. Always love how that dress matches your eyes."

Her eyes? The door to her room latched shut behind her grandmother and Siobhan studied the dress draped across the bed. A beautiful emerald green sheath dress, with one side off the shoulder. The problem at hand, she didn't want to accentuate her eyes, she wanted Jack to swallow his tongue. Taking a second look in her closet, she'd been to plenty of black-tie events in the family requiring a floor-length gown, but none had been meant to attract a man's attention. A real man.

Shaking her head, she knew she needed help. And fast. Her cell in hand, Siobhan called the only person who knew Jack as well as her brothers. Unite and conquer. Jack Preston had no idea what he was in for.

Even though Jack had arrived early to snatch a few minutes with Siobhan's brothers before she arrived, the crowds for the popular senator were already surrounding Mitch. Neither Kyle nor Craig were in town for the event, which meant only Mitch and Chase were present. If he could win them over, convincing Kyle and Craig not to run him out of town on a rail would be easier. Except, maybe this hadn't been his brightest idea. The two brothers were currently at opposite ends of the ballroom and Jack had no idea how to corral them without tipping his hand.

Swirling the ginger ale in his glass, Jack blew out a soft sigh. Bourbon was his favored drink, but if his plan was to convince the Baron men that he was a good choice for sweet Siobhan, somehow ginger ale seemed more appropriate. Though a little liquid courage before telling her brothers his intentions held a great deal of appeal at the moment. The key to the conversation was to be clear and aboveboard with everyone.

Glancing at his watch, anticipation of Siobhan's arrival battled with anxiousness over his upcoming conversation with the Baron men. Spotting a break in the circle of supporters surrounding Mitch, Jack swallowed the last drop of soda, set the glass on the bar and strode over to Mitch. Mitch's more serious nature would make him the hardest sell. It made sense to start with him. If Jack could get Mitch on board, the rest of the brothers would hopefully fall into step like a trail of dominoes.

"Hey, Jack." Mitch gave his friend a casual slap on the arm, too friendly for a handshake, not the right setting for a man hug. "Always good to see a friendly face at these events."

"From what I can see, you've got more than enough friendly faces."

Mitch shook his head. "Don't let the smiles fool you. Everyone here wants something from me."

The darkness in his eyes and the weight of his tone had Jack second-guessing his plan.

"If you've got some hidden legislation on the back of your mind, I'm telling you now. Not interested."

"What?" Wrapped up in his own thoughts, he failed to connect the dots of the conversation.

"Sorry." Mitch shook his head. "It gets old, everyone wanting something. Every time I turn around. You look serious. Is something wrong?"

"No. Not wrong." This was where he had to find the right words. "I do want to talk to you about something, in private."

"There you are." A balding man with a belly that looked ready to bust out of the cummerbund, slapped Mitch on the back and sloshed a bit of liquid over the rim of his drinking glass. The night was starting early. "I hear you're still sitting on that legislation we discussed at the last event."

"Well—" Mitch forced a smile, but Busting

Cummerbund cut him off.

"I'll do you a favor and save you the trouble of repeating yourself. Wentworth and some of your other supporters are as anxious as I am for an update. Let's join them at the table."

Before Jack could react, Mitch was whisked away to a table clear across the room. At this rate, he had no choice but to seek out Chase. Smiling at the other bar in the ballroom with his wife at his side, the other brother seemed to be in a better mood. Taking in a fortified breath, Jack strode across the ballroom as casually as he could without breaking into a run.

Chase leaned against the bar as if marking Jack's progress across the room. "Hey, buddy." Not up for re-election, Chase didn't hesitate to offer that one-armed bro hug that men did. "Ready for a refill?"

"Ginger ale for me."

Chase's eyes rounded like a cartoon caricature. "Say again?"

"Ginger ale."

"Not feeling well?" Chase teased.

Did everyone expect Jack to always drink? He might have to rethink his image if he survived tonight. "I'm doing fine. Thanks."

Chase studied Jack. "Markets good? Do we need to juggle some investments?"

"No." He shook his head. Jack didn't want to do small talk. "Markets are good, but what I really want is to chat a minute about Siobhan."

"Oh. I see Paige. I'll let you two knights in shining armor have at it." CJ, who'd been chatting with another woman at the bar, gave her husband, then Jack, a peck on the cheek and crossed the room to where Paige and Eve had come in.

"She's right." Chase lifted his chin in his departing wife's direction. "We owe you a thanks for rescuing Siobhan today."

"Glad I was available."

"You think there was something to those guys?"

"I think the world is filled with bad people and, yeah, they may have been a couple of them."

Chase frowned and Jack knew exactly how the guy felt. It had taken Jack a while to stop stewing over what could have gone wrong had he not arrived when he did.

"Like I said, thanks."

"Nothing to thank me for. I care about her too." What Jack needed but didn't have, was time to soften Chase up, ease him into the conversation about the little sister that wasn't so little anymore. Not that Jack blamed any of them for being protective of her, Siobhan wasn't his sister and he felt the exact same way. "Which brings me around to something we need to discuss before Siobhan arrives."

Nodding, Chase reached for the ginger ale the bartender had served and handed it over to Jack. "I'm all ears. But if you want me to reel in our baby sister, you're jack out of luck—no pun intended. That kid has a mind and adrenaline tolerance that's all Baron and hard to control."

"She's definitely all Baron, but there's no baby or kid in her. Not anymore."

That had Chase frowning again. Whether the guy was doing math in his head or preparing to argue, Jack had no idea, because his eyeballs suddenly popped in conjunction with the low whistles of a few men at the bar. "What the…"

A guy Jack didn't recognize elbowed Chase. "Looks like your little sister isn't so little anymore."

"Watch it," Chase and Jack chorused.

That made the line between Chase's brows deepen.

Jack sighed. Knowing the second he turned around and saw Siobhan, how he felt would be painted all over his face for Chase and anyone else paying attention to see, this wasn't going to be easy.

"Crap." Chase rolled his eyes. "Why do they have to grow up? That kid, no, that *woman* is going to break some hearts tonight. Right after I punch a few of them in the nose first."

And if he guessed right, Jack's nose would be the first to make contact with Chase's fist.

A matching deep-set frown between his brows, Mitch

appeared beside his brother. "When the hell did Siobhan start dressing like a vixen?"

"First of all, no one uses the word vixen anymore; secondly, I believe it's called growing up." Chase's gaze narrowed. "And I don't like it one bit."

"Which brings me back to what I wanted to discuss with you two," Jack interjected.

"Not now." Chase pushed away from the bar. "I need to run interference."

"Right behind you." Mitch straightened his tie and Jack dared to spin around.

Holy… All the breath in his lungs left him. Donning a strapless royal blue dress that showed more assets than he liked, Siobhan closed the distance between them. From the way just about every male eye in the room turned her way, he wasn't the only one to notice her…assets. A thin strand of pearls hung around a long kissable neck and rested just above a hint of exposed cleavage. Enough flesh to taunt a man's imagination and tease his sanity. The tight swath of fabric draped about a narrow waist showcased an hour glass figure. With each step across the crowded ballroom, the clinging fabric swished back and forth, a single slit just above the knee exposing long, shapely legs. Legs that were doing as much to fuel his imagination as the rest of her.

"Hi." Siobhan came to a stop in front of him, and completely ignoring her brothers, laid one hand on his forearm and leaned in for the tiniest of pecks on the lips. Not his cheek as she might have done only a few short years ago, but smack on the lips.

"Hi," he managed to mutter back, just in time to see Eve half a step behind her smiling, and not one but two Baron brothers staring daggers at him.

No matter how he sliced it, he was in so much trouble.

CHAPTER THIRTEEN

Siobhan had no idea which was more entertaining, the shock on Jack's face as she did her best to strut across the ballroom, or that just-sucked-on-a-lemon look on Mitch and Chase's faces. When Eve swore on her favorite chocolate martini that this was the dress that would knock Jack off his feet, Siobhan had her doubts. She really liked the red dress with the drop back or the gold dress with the sweetheart neckline. All Eve did was shake her head and point to the deep royal blue option over and over.

She could still hear Eve repeating, "Jack's a leg man. The peek of leg on the side slit will drive him crazy. The cleavage won't hurt, he is a man after all, but it's the leg he only gets a hint of that will drive him nuts."

Time would tell if Eve was right.

"Isn't there a shawl or wrap that goes with that dress?" Chase didn't know where to look. Every time his gaze dropped to her neckline or bare shoulders, it immediately shot back up to her face.

It took everything in her not to laugh.

"If it had one, she'd be wearing it." Eve actually rolled her eyes at their brothers.

Mitch glared at their sister. "Whose side are you on?"

"I don't take sides." Eve reached for her brother, the senator's, hand. "Come on. I like this song. Let's dance before all the rich women in the room claim you."

"But…" Keeping his eyes on Siobhan, he was practically digging his heels in as Eve dragged him onto the floor.

"There you are." Paige appeared beside her brother. "I love this song. Let's dance."

Chase whipped his head left at Paige then back to Siobhan before scowling at Jack. "Later."

"This song will be over later." Sticking her arm straight out, Paige snatched Chase's hand. "Come on, big brother. Make your sister happy."

Still scowling, he shifted his gaze from Siobhan to Jack as Paige dragged him into the middle of the floor beside Mitch and Eve. Bless her big sisters. They understood what Siobhan was going through and how hard it was to force her brothers to view her as a woman fully grown and not the baby of the family.

"Shall we?" Jack held his elbow out to her.

She couldn't stop the smile from taking over her face. "I'd love to."

Together, they slowly strolled across the wooden floor to the center of the dance area. As if they'd been dancing together their entire lives, his hand wound around her waist and the other hand enfolded hers in his. One step back and in seconds they were gliding around the room like Fred and Ginger. Another minute and doing something equivalent to a fancy two-step, Jack twirled her in place before pulling her back into his arms. She couldn't help but chuckle and smile up at him.

From the corner of her eye, she spotted Mitch, his lips pressed tightly together, shooting daggers at Jack. Another twirl around the floor and Chase had maneuvered his way over to them. Just like her other brother, Chase silently scolded Jack with his piercing scowl. Not wanting to laugh out loud at her brothers, she buried her head in Jack's shoulder, muffling her laughter.

"Are you trying to get me killed?" Jack teased.

Without moving away, she shook her head against him. "I can hear your heartbeat."

She also felt him swallow and suck in a deep breath. Instantly his heartbeat slowed. "That's probably a good thing, because I'm pretty sure it stopped when you walked into the room."

Barely inching back, she lifted her face to see his eyes. "Really?"

Chuckling slightly, he nodded. "Most definitely. You, Siobhan Baron, are a knockout. And if you haven't noticed, you're driving me crazy."

"I think I like that." Smothering a smile, she leaned against him again.

To her surprise, at no point did Jack make an effort to stop dancing. The music went through a few ballads before switching to a couple of faster tunes. Mitch had indeed been pulled away by one wealthy patron after another. Chase, on the other hand, had approached them more than once, clearly intending to cut in before Paige or Eve stepped in and steered him away to dance.

"The waitstaff is serving dinner."

Jack glanced across the room to where their table was. "We should probably go sit."

"Would it be out of place for me to say, I don't want to let you go?"

His head dipped and he very gently kissed her temple. "Ditto."

"So what do we do?"

"I had hoped to talk to your brothers before you arrived. Since that didn't happen, I can't promise there won't be a scene when we go sit."

Taking a minute to scope out where her two siblings were, she spotted Mitch deeply engrossed in conversation with some old coot. Chase had taken a seat at the table, not beside their grandparents, but a seat away so that she and Jack would not be able to sit side by side.

"I suppose we should face the music." Even though sitting at the table with her annoyed brothers was the last thing she wanted to do.

"That would be the adult thing to do." His eyes sparkled with amusement and without his saying a word, she knew exactly what he was thinking.

"Or," she smiled up at him, "we could sneak out."

"If we're going to do this..." He paused to gingerly kiss the top of her head before continuing. "We're going to have to face them sooner or later."

"This?" She hadn't meant for her voice to sound so

small and insecure.

"Us." His words came out low and husky and her toes almost curled in her shoes.

The single word put a smile on her face. "I like the sound of that."

"Then we face the music?"

Her gaze drifted to the table where Mitch had joined their grandparents and other siblings and slowly shook her head. "I vote for escape."

"Whatever the lady wants." The twinkle in his eyes dimmed momentarily behind a heavy curtain of emotions she couldn't quite read before the corners of his lips tipped north into a lazy smile. "They're going to be mad as hell at us."

"Yes." She took a step in retreat, already bemoaning the loss of his heat against her, but didn't let go of the one hand that had been holding hers as they'd danced. Looking around him, she grinned broadly. "Isn't that just a shame?"

The only thing Jack wanted to do while standing at the curb waiting for the valet to bring his car around, was pull Siobhan into his arms and kiss her until neither could take another breath. That, of course, would not be his best idea yet. For now, holding her hand tightly in his was going to have to do.

Except for the few moments after the valet brought the car around and Jack had to leave Siobhan in the passenger seat of his classic corvette, he had not let go of her hand. For whatever reason, he needed that connection. The bigger problem for him, though, would be leaving her at the front door. All of this was insane. He'd been infatuated before. Even considered himself in love a time or two. Though most would consider his obsession with his ninth-grade English teacher more puppy love than in love. However, the truth was, he'd never in his life wanted to be with a woman every second of the day, and he had no clue how to handle the flood of emotions swirling around in his chest, squeezing his pounding heart.

They'd made it the entire drive to the ranch with only a moment or two of comfortable silence, usually when Siobhan raised the volume on the radio, dancing in her seat and belting out one tune or other. They'd carefully managed to avoid any mention of Mitch or Chase's reaction, or of what would happen when they spoke to Kyle and Craig. Instead, they chatted easily about everything and anything, including the upcoming show. The excitement that danced in her eyes as she told him all about her meeting with Veronica was totally contagious. Only for a moment when she mentioned wishing her mother could be here for the upcoming event did the excitement dim, quickly returning as she described Veronica's positive reactions to her photos. To his surprise, the delight at her happiness was the biggest high he'd ever experienced. Suddenly, he was completely sure of his intentions for Siobhan, intentions he would share with her overly protective brothers. More than anything in this world, he wanted to make Siobhan his wife. The only thing that seemed to scare him was the thought that she might not want the same thing. He'd have to proceed with caution. The last thing he wanted was to scare her away with professions of undying love and devotion. Man, didn't he sound like a love-struck teenager.

"Careful!" Siobhan screeched at the same second he spotted the car without headlights speeding past them on the narrow dirt road leading to the ranch. "What the heck is the matter with those people?"

"I'm going to guess someone drank their dinner."

Sitting upright in the passenger seat, Siobhan shook her head. "Should we call 911?"

"No point. They were driving so fast, by the time an officer is dispatched, they'll be long gone."

She sank back into the seat. "You're right. I know that, but it irks me to let them get away."

And there was another thing he'd grown to love about Siobhan, her strong sense of fair play.

Turning into the driveway, he debated what excuse he

could come up with to stay a little longer. He had no idea if Chase or Mitch were coming back to the ranch. All the members of the family, except Siobhan, had their own homes in Texas, but until recently when they started marrying, most of them spent more time at the ranch than their own places. Understanding exactly how he felt, and the future he wanted, staying to chat with the Governor if no one else might be a smart idea. Then again, if they stayed till the end of the benefit, the middle of the night might not be the best time for a civil discussion of any kind.

At a stop in front of the massive family home, Jack trotted around the hood to open the car door for Siobhan.

"Thank you." She pushed to her feet and gave him a sweet but too-brief kiss on the lips. "Come in for a night cap or coffee?"

"Coffee." He smiled, following her up the front steps.

Staring at the door, she nudged the door open. "That's odd. I could have sworn I pulled it shut behind me when I left."

"Maybe one of the household staff left it open?"

She shook her head. "No, they all left for their night off before me."

"Wait." Odds were she simply had not pulled the door shut all the way, but he didn't want her walking into a burglary in progress. "I'll go in first. Let you know if it's okay."

The frown already at home on her forehead deepened before she quietly nodded.

Carefully scanning the foyer, he listened for any sounds of intruders, gesturing for her to remain at the front door. Sticking his head into the front parlor first, nothing seemed out of place. Next he looked at the dining room. All the large sterling silver pieces appeared in place. Any burglar worth his salt would know that the candelabras on the table alone were probably worth five figures. The knots in his stomach eased and he reentered the hall. "I think it's okay."

Relief washed away Siobhan's concern. "Good, because I don't know the combo to the gun safe."

Jack rolled his eyes at her. If there'd been burglars in

the house, there would have been no time to go hunting for a gun in a safe.

"Coffee?" She stood in front of him.

Narrowing his gaze, he looked across the hall to the Governor's study. "Did you leave the lights on in the study?"

She shook her head. "No."

"Someone did."

CHAPTER FOURTEEN

"**I** liked it better when you said everything was okay." The look of concern on Siobhan's face brought out every protective instinct Jack had.

With her plastered against his back, he slowly entered the study. To his eye, everything looked in place. Watching where he stepped, he circled the desk. A couple of drawers were slightly open. He couldn't imagine the former Marine patriarch not being precise about everything, including closing desk drawers.

"Hmm." Siobhan stepped around him to the wall of bookshelves. "Someone knocked this over."

She leaned over and Jack grabbed her arm. "Don't touch that. Just in case."

"So someone was here?" Her voice didn't quite crack, but came close. She was putting up a brave front.

"Maybe. And maybe you should call the Governor and give him a heads up."

"And then call the police." Those nerves of steel he knew her to have were resurfacing.

He shook his head. "Better see what your grandfather wants to do first."

With a nod of her head, Siobhan pulled her cell out of the glittery small purse still dangling from her arm and called the Governor.

Jack eyed the room carefully, looking for any additional sign of an intruder, or a really bad housemaid.

"Okay." Siobhan tossed her phone onto the desk. "Grams and the Governor are already on their way home. The chicken was dry and the music got too loud."

Her delivery of why the Barons were on their way home

actually made him chuckle despite the potential severity of the situation. "I suggest we wait in the other room."

"Sounds good. You make yourself at home, I'm going to run upstairs and change into something more comfortable, then I'll make that pot of coffee I offered you."

Following her toward the stairway, he nodded. "Tell you what. Why don't you go change and I'll put on the coffee?"

She leaned forward and quickly kissed his cheek. "A man of many talents."

All he could think was how many more of his talents he wished he could show her. He hadn't been in the kitchen more than a minute when a blood-curdling scream reached his ears. *Siobhan.* Damn it. Dropping the pot in the sink, he bolted down the hall and up the stairs. He should have checked the whole house before assuming all was well.

Barreling down the second-floor hall, he took the turn into her room without slowing down, grabbing onto the doorway for balance. In the middle of the bedroom Siobhan stood, her hands on her mouth, surrounded by piles of… everything.

As neat as the Governor's office looked, Siobhan's room did not. Drawers in her dressers and vanity were wide open, contents dumped on the floor. Even the bedsheets and spread had been pulled back and dangled off the foot of the bed. Night table drawers were open, books had been pulled away from one wall of shelves. A tripod and some other equipment bags he recognized from the wedding were thrown on top of a pile of sweaters.

"Why?" she muttered softly, before spinning around and almost falling into his arms.

Cradling her as tightly as he dared, he whispered over her head, "I don't know, but you're all right. That's what matters."

She bobbed her head against his shoulder. "I don't want to think what would have happened if I'd been home alone."

Neither did he. The thought had him pulling her tighter against him. Standing here in the middle of this bedroom carnage wasn't helping his or her nerves, but before he could suggest waiting for the Governor downstairs, her gaze lifted to meet his and all sanity slid away. It didn't matter that the Barons had been burglarized or that Siobhan's room was targeted. Beautiful, pink, plump lips called to him. Leaning in, he kissed her the way he'd wanted to all night.

"Siobhan?" The Governor's voice carried up the stairs, followed by multiple sets of footsteps.

He knew he should back away, stop, catch his breath, but he needed just one more second. And then a lifetime.

"What the hell?" the Governor's voice boomed.

Who separated first, him or her, he wasn't sure, but he took another step in retreat, loosening his hold of Siobhan, but not fully letting go.

The next thing he knew, before he or Siobhan could say a word, Chase's voice bellowed through the small room. "Son of a ..."

A hard grip pulled him into a spin about two seconds before a very firm, angry fist slammed into his jaw.

"Chase!" The single name ripped from her throat louder than the scream at the sight of her room. "What the hell are you doing?"

Fists clenched at his side, Chase's gaze darted to the unmade bed and back to Jack. "You have one helluva a nerve coming into our home—"

"Stop," the Governor ordered. "Have you taken a good look at the room?"

"It's a mess." Chase continued to glare at Jack.

"Chase." Grams' hand settled gently on her grandson's arm. "Your sister is upset that someone has violated her room."

"From where I stand, more than her room has been violated." Chase seemed to be daring Jack to give him a reason for taking another swing.

To her surprise, Jack simply stood there, almost bracing

himself for the next punch.

"Chase," the Governor repeated, "call the police. Obviously, we've been burglarized."

Like a glass of cold water to the face, the Governor's words had Chase looking around the room more slowly, and then his eyes settled on Siobhan, still in the beautiful but snug evening gown. Sucking in a deep breath and slowly blowing it out, he nodded. "I'll call the police." Pausing in the doorway, he waved a finger at Jack. "I may have overreacted, but I'm not wrong. We need to talk."

Jack bobbed his chin.

"If there's anything that hasn't been thrown on the floor," Grams scanned the mess, "you might want to go ahead, change clothes, and join us downstairs."

"Yes, ma'am." Getting out of this sausage stuffing dress sounded great, but she didn't want to leave Jack's side. Not knowing what else to do or say, she reached out and grabbed hold of his hand.

The stern expression on his face slipped away. His gaze lowered to meet hers and he managed a weak smile. "I'll wait for you in the hall."

"You owe him an apology." If there was one thing that James Ernest Baron was good at, it was judging character. He could not have had a successful military and political career without it. "He was consoling and caring for your sister."

"He was kissing her," Chase practically spat.

"That too." His beloved Lila smiled at their grandson.

"She's our baby sister."

Lila handed Chase a short glass of bourbon she'd poured for him. "She may be your youngest sister, but there's nothing baby about her."

Accepting the glass, Chase sighed. "She's too young."

"For what?" Lila asked.

When it came to matters of the heart, James had learned

a very long time ago to let his wife take the lead.

"Everything." Chase took a slow sip of his drink.

Lila shook her head. "She's a legal adult well past twenty-one."

"He's too old for her."

That made the Governor chuckle. He too was a decade older than his wife, but he kept his mouth shut.

The sound of muffled laughter from his grandfather gave Chase pause. Both James and Lila could easily tell the moment their grandson had done the math in his head and made the connection. "That's different."

"Why?" Lila didn't mince words.

Chase stared into his drink as if the ice cubes held a secret code before shaking his head. "It just is."

"Is there something wrong with Jack?" Lila continued.

"Of course not." For the first time in the conversation, Chase almost looked repentant.

"So he's a good man?"

Reluctantly, Chase nodded.

"Hard worker?"

Another nod.

"A good friend?"

"You know he is." Chase draped his hand behind his neck. "It's just Siobhan. I don't want her to be another notch on his bedpost. She's a good kid."

"I believe," James spoke up, "your grandmother has reminded you, she's not a kid."

"Fine." Tension returned to Chase's shoulders. "I don't want my grown-up sister to be another notch on his bedpost."

"While I agree with you," Lila reached over to scratch behind the ears of Honey who had come to sit beside her, "I apparently have more faith in your sister *and* your friend than you do."

"Anyone who goes after my sister isn't the friend I thought he was."

"All right." Lila continued to scratch the dog's ears. "What was the name of that young man who followed our Siobhan around like a puppy?"

"Dwayne," James replied.

"What about him?" Lila leveled her gaze with Chase's. "Would he be better for your sister?"

"That pimply-faced kid wouldn't know what to do with an electric bill if it bit him on the as…butt."

Lila smiled. "Very well. Maybe that fellow she dated her senior year of college. The one who wanted her to join him in the mountains of South America to work with the indigenous tribes."

"She *was* smitten with him," James added.

"That would fade fast after her first case of Montezuma's revenge."

"I believe that's Mexico." James tried not to laugh at his grandson's struggles to justify his actions—and misguided opinions.

Chase set his empty glass on the table beside him. "Whatever."

For a short moment, Lila and James exchanged glances.

It was clear to him that his wife felt she'd made her point. Waiting a long few moments before speaking again, "Perhaps you should ask your sister what she thinks of Jack."

"I know what she thinks. She was kissing him."

Lila bobbed her head. "Very well. Then perhaps the one you need to talk to is Jack. Without your fists. After all, he's the only one who knows his intentions."

His hands clasped in front of him, James leaned forward on his seat. "I admit, at first the idea of a man of Jack's reputation with your youngest sister did not sit well with me."

"See." Chase sat back in the seat and dropped his ankle over his knee.

"But." James held up a finger. "Someone," he gazed pointedly at his wife smiling across the room, "reminded me of my youthful reputation as a ladies' man before I fell in love with your grandmother. And frankly, I don't think a younger man would be man enough for someone with a spirit like your sister's."

Chase's jaw tightened and James could almost hear his

teeth grinding as he pondered his grandfather's words.

At the same time Siobhan and Jack's footsteps could be heard coming down the stairs, the doorbell rang.

"That must be the police." Lila looked to her husband.

"I'll get the door." James pushed to his feet and passed Siobhan and Jack at the foot of the stairs. Opening the door to the officers, he paid more attention to what Chase was doing. From where he stood in front of the study while the officers carefully stepped inside, he could see Chase come to a stop beside his friend. At least that was a start.

Another few awkward moments later and his hands behind his back and his gaze focused on the study door, Chase leaned into his friend and muttered, "If you screw with her, it'll be the last thing you ever do."

The Governor almost laughed at the not so veiled threat. One grandson down and three more to convince. Somehow dealing with raw recruits seemed easier. He just hoped his lovely wife was right about all this—again.

CHAPTER FIFTEEN

The last several days had been a bit like walking on eggs around her brothers. Between the news of the break-in and Chase's altercation with Jack, one by one the other three had shown up at the ranch. The police had made fast work of checking for fingerprints wherever there were signs of an intruder. In the end, all the prints belonged to either family or household staff, but the police were sure the front door had been jimmied open. The officers had suggested not leaving the dogs kenneled when the house was empty, though her grandmother didn't seem to like that idea.

By the next day, the family had opted to improve security and chalked the intrusion off as just one of those things. Unfortunately, that meant more time to focus on her and Jack. At every given opportunity, she'd done her best to convince the three that she knew exactly what she was doing and that Jack was as good as any of them. She had no idea what any or all of them had said to Jack in private, but for now Jack's efforts seemed to have gone a long way to appease her brothers. Whatever challenges the three Baron men might come up with later on in their relationship—she actually smiled to herself at the word *relationship*; she was in a relationship with Jack Preston—for now, there was a tentative truce. If nothing else, no one threatened to punch Jack when he picked her up this morning to meet with Veronica at the gallery. Unlike previous days, neither Mitch nor Craig, the only two brothers here this morning, even looked like they wanted to slug him. That was definitely real progress.

Since she had no idea how long this final decision

session with Veronica would take, Jack had left her at the door and gone to run a few errands of his own. Now, her photos were spread out over a large table so both she and Veronica could eye them together.

"The composition is amazing on these two." Her fingers tapping one of the photographs, Veronica looked pointedly at Siobhan. "Did you get releases?"

Siobhan shook her head. "No. I was focusing on the tattered playground equipment. I didn't realize there were people in the background."

The gallery owner blew out a soft sigh. "Too bad there are people."

Siobhan pressed her lips tightly together to hide her disappointment. The photos were two of her favorites. Had these prints been for commercial use, and not an artist's showing, she would have simply cropped out the people. When she was in the groove, when a subject had her complete interest, she didn't notice anything else.

"This one would be my next favorite." Veronica gestured at the photo of the little girl laughing on the carousel. "Do you have a release for this?"

Waving her hand in a so-so gesture, she reluctantly nodded. "At the time I didn't have one handy, but I have the mother's contact info and she's willing to sign."

"Now we're making progress. I'd like to have it in hand, but if the mother does sign, I'm sure this shot will be very popular. I might even want to make it the centerpiece of the display."

Even though Veronica seemed very pleased to use that photo for the foundation of the exhibit, as each acceptable photograph was set to one side, Siobhan's gaze kept returning to the discarded two. One in particular she was especially proud of. How had she not noticed people in the distance? If their backs had been to the camera she could have ignored it, but one of the people had been looking straight at her.

Next in the stack of prints were the ones she'd taken that day with her friend, Bridget. Siobhan held her breath as Veronica shifted around the prints, finally bobbing her head, tapping her finger on the lone flower blooming among the boulders. "Now this one makes so much sense in contrast with the more gritty city photos." She added it to the other shots that had made the final cut.

So far, so good. Despite Veronica's satisfaction with most of the photos, a startling chill nipped at Siobhan. Rubbing her arms to chase the feeling away, she lifted her gaze and looked out the front window. Ever since the break-in, things hadn't felt completely right. The whole situation had made her a little jumpy and she didn't like it.

"These." The gallery owner waved her arm and grinned, a beam of pride in her eyes as though she'd been the one to take the photos and not Siobhan.

Siobhan looked over the prints the woman had picked and something clicked. "I see a theme."

"Exactly." Now Veronica was truly grinning like the Cheshire Cat.

The rumble of an engine drew her attention away from Veronica and the prints. A sleek sports car pulled up in front of the gallery. The mere sight of Jack made her almost giddy.

Veronica glanced up at the car now parked in front. "I noticed Jack Preston dropped you off earlier."

Siobhan couldn't hide her smile. "Yes."

"Haven't seen as much of him in the papers lately. He seems to be keeping a lower profile."

Not knowing what else to say, she simply shrugged.

"I remember once after one of your brother Kyle's races, the two had been photographed all night—and morning—in different bars, and always with a passel of beautiful women at their sides."

Her brother and Jack partying around the world was nothing new. The two had been close friends for as long as she could remember. Both were richer than Croesus and romance book cover handsome. Paparazzi had followed them around like puppy dogs.

"So he's finally settling down?" Veronica asked.

"I guess." What else could she say?

"You seem smitten."

Heat rushed to her cheeks, but she couldn't drag her eyes away from Jack as he climbed out of the car, circled the hood, and the moment their gazes met, waved at her through the front window. His grin as large as hers.

"Apparently, the feeling is mutual."

She spun around to see the knowing grin on the gallery owner's face. For sure, Siobhan's cheeks were burning warm. Blasted Irish skin. Always betraying her when she blushed.

Veronica shrugged. "Jack's quite the catch. If you decide you don't want him, there's a line of women willing to step into your shoes."

"Nope." There was no way she was letting this one get away. No matter how much her brothers puffed out their chests and snarled at him, Jack Preston was hers and she had no intention of letting him go.

"Hey." Jack paused at the door, waved at Veronica then waited for Siobhan to signal if they were finished or not.

That was another thing she loved about Jack, unlike her overbearing brothers, he always respected her space, and right now, her career. She knew he would not interrupt her work.

"I guess we're all set." Veronica gestured to the stack of keeper prints. "You've got the dates, and you're in charge of framing them."

"Everything will be ready." It might be a push, but she'd get it done. This showing would be perfect.

The meeting clearly finished, Jack approached the two.

"Nice to see you again, Jack." Veronica extended her arm.

Shaking the proffered hand, he seamlessly slid his other arm around Siobhan's waist sending delighted tingles up her spine. She loved the gentle almost territorial gesture. "Always love coming to events here. I'm looking forward to Siobhan's show."

"So am I." Veronica nodded. "I'm expecting a lot of buzz, but bring all your friends. And tell them to bring their checkbooks." She laughed.

Checkbooks. Wow. Not till this moment had it actually

struck Siobhan that this was about more than exposure, this show could make her money. A lot of it.

Everyone said their goodbyes, and still arm in arm, she and Jack crossed the short distance to the car. Another chilled breeze passed over her and she paused, looking around.

"You okay?" Holding the car door open for her, Jack's smile slipped.

"You ever get the feeling you're being watched?"

His gaze raked up and down the street. Seeing the same empty sidewalks she had, his smile returned. "Sometimes, but it's usually my mother staring daggers at me for forgetting something she'd drummed into me in my youth."

That made Siobhan laugh. She knew exactly the kind of look he meant. Not that she'd ever seen his mother scolding him with her eyes, but her own mother and grandmother had done so on more than one occasion.

Taking another second to scan the street, she heaved a contented sigh. Life was good, if only she could get over the jumpy feeling.

In the short time he'd been spending with Siobhan, he'd come to trust her instincts as much as his own. He slid into the car and studied her. "Why do you ask?"

She frowned and then shrugged. "I don't know, just a funny feeling I can't seem to shake. I guess that stupid break-in and no real answers from the police has left me a little unnerved."

It was his turn to frown. He looked up and down the street again, but saw nothing suspicious. "I know this has to be hard on you and your family, but you have a lot of people who care about you and are there to keep you safe." He squeezed her hand. "That includes me."

Her head bobbed and the sweetest smile made his heart happy. He smiled back and started the car. "Next stop, the ranch."

Normally the first thing she'd do in his car was mess with the radio, then she'd be bouncing around, or talking at him a mile a minute about something that had her all excited. All week the show had been top on the list. As he walked to the gallery from his car a short while ago, he could see the sheer joy on her face as she spoke with Veronica.

Now, in a matter of minutes, all the fire in her soul seemed to have slipped away. "What's wrong?"

She shrugged and leaned her head back against the seat. "I just wish my brothers could see I'm not a baby any more."

At least she wasn't upset with anything he'd done or said. "Give them time. They'll come around."

"That's what I'm afraid of."

"That they'll come around?" What had he missed?

Chuckling, a hint of light reappeared in her eyes. "Giving them time. I have visions of getting their blessing to date you on my fiftieth birthday."

Now, he was the one to laugh. "Maybe not that much time." Without thinking, he reached over and covered her hand with his. He'd been doing this all week, and today, it occurred to him that he'd never dated a woman in his entire life whose hand he craved to hold. Never had he felt the need to feel connected, even if only by the touch of fingertips.

"Okay. Now you've got a funny look on your face. Is it one of my brothers? Because so help me, if they're giving you more grief again, I'll knock their lights out."

"Whoa, Champ. Your brothers have been very civil."

"I'm not looking for civil. I'm looking for normal."

So was he. Chase was slowly coming around, Mitch was hard to read. Craig seemed to be on the fence, but Kyle was a tough nut to crack. The two of them had sowed many an oat in their years of friendship and he could only begin to imagine what Kyle must think. Heaven knew if Jack had a kid sister dating the old Kyle Baron, Jack would be anything but happy.

By the time they'd parked in front of the ranch house

and made their way inside, the house was buzzing with activity. Jack had known most of the Baron cousins since childhood. After all, Kyle was his oldest and bestest friend. But what Jack hadn't expected was the warm welcome from most of the cousins.

Leah Baron had dragged Siobhan away to look at who knew what, while Devlin had cornered him about a new real estate project he had on the table. As Dev was called away by his sister Claire, he paused and slapped Jack on the back. "For the record, I think you and Siobhan are good for each other."

Before Jack could form a thought, Devlin had walked away, leaving him standing alone in the foyer.

"Don't look so confused." Smiling at him, Eve, his former plus one and Siobhan's older sister, shook her head and sidled up beside him. "Kyle doesn't speak for the whole family."

"Then you're okay with Siobhan and me, too?"

"Whose blue dress do you think she wore last weekend?"

He couldn't help but smile at Eve. "Thank you."

"Don't let my stubborn brothers bother you. We're working on them. It'll be fine."

"I'm taking things really slowly, but when it comes to Siobhan, I seem to be a little short on patience." Kyle and Mitch were holding strong in their unwillingness to bend, proving the hardest to convince of his intentions.

Eve leaned back, eyed him carefully, and bobbed her head. "I never thought I'd see the day anyone would domesticate Jack Preston, the most eligible bachelor in Houston. I'd better work on Kyle a little harder."

"Mitch too, please." Pandering for any help in his efforts to convince the Baron men that he wasn't toying with their sister's affections wasn't beneath him.

With a quick peck on his cheek, and a sweet smile that reminded him of Siobhan, she took a step in retreat. "But just to be clear, if you break her heart—"

"It'll be the last thing I ever do. I'm getting that message loud and clear."

Her grin widened and she patted his arm. "As long as we understand each other."

Looking around, he found himself searching for Siobhan. Eve was right. The Jack Preston standing in the foyer was not the same guy who had partied hard with Kyle and company. Somehow, he had to prove that to Siobhan's brothers. And the way he felt, sooner would be better than later.

CHAPTER SIXTEEN

The day of the gallery show had finally arrived. Siobhan had barely slept last night. The chosen prints were all framed and delivered to the gallery a few days ago. Under the wire, but delivered. Veronica wouldn't let her see the display and curiosity was driving Siobhan crazy.

"Maybe a stiff brandy will help," the Governor teased, but deep down, she suspected he was actually serious.

"I'll be fine."

"What you're going to do is burst a blood vessel if you don't relax." Her grandmother patted her arm and slung her purse over her shoulder. "Are you sure you don't want us to give you a ride?

"Jack should be here any second."

A smile tugged at the older woman's mouth. "I am truly happy you two are growing so close, but it's a shame to have made him come all the way up here when he lives not far from the gallery."

Of course her grandmother was right, and Siobhan had insisted she could catch a ride with any number of people, but Jack was adamant that he pick her up and escort her himself.

"And speaking of your escort." Grams grinned at the Governor. "I guess you're in good hands now."

"Governor, Mrs. Baron." Jack came to a stop at the open front door. Casual greetings were exchanged and her grandparents climbed into their car.

Jack's gaze drifted over her shoulder. "Anyone else home?"

"Just us."

A smile as wide as the Rio Grande took over his face and lit up his eyes. "In that case."

Before she could catch her breath, he'd scooped her into his arms and had done more for her raw nerves in a single kiss than all the pacing and deep breathing had done in the last two days.

Slowly easing back, Jack blew out a deep sigh and without letting go of her hands, took another step in retreat. "You ready?"

"As ready as I'll ever be."

"You're going to knock it out of the ball park. You'll see."

She really hoped he was right. As Grams used to say, she was more nervous than a long-tailed cat in a room full of rockers. "I don't know why I'm so on edge. I keep reminding myself the prints are good, but I can't help feeling like a fraud, getting by on the family name."

"Nonsense. You're incredibly gifted and after today, all of Houston will know it."

"From your mouth to God's ears." She slid into a lightweight shawl and followed Jack to the car.

The ride to the gallery was made in near silence. Only the tight grip of Jack's hand on hers kept her from crawling out of her skin. At least the nerves had shifted from concern to anticipation.

Jack pulled into the parking at the rear of the gallery and together they walked around to the front door.

"There's the woman of the hour." Eve and Paige were helping set up the bar with champagne and wines from the Baron Vineyard.

Veronica looked down at her watch and shook her head. "You're not supposed to be here for another thirty minutes." Moving forward, the gallery owner took Siobhan by the hand and gently spun her around. "Why don't you go take a short walk while we finish up here."

The words had gone in one ear and fallen out of the other. She couldn't stop staring at her photos hanging on the wall under specialty lights. "Oh, boy."

"Oh, boy is right." Veronica shook her head and

redirected Siobhan and Jack. "Jack, I think the waitstaff and Siobhan's sisters could use a little help unloading the wine."

Paige leaned in and spoke up at him. "The winery van broke down so we're running a bit late. The extra hands wouldn't hurt."

"I can pitch in." Siobhan shoved the sleeves of her blouse up over her elbow.

"Nope." Veronica shook her head. "You go take some nice photos in the neighborhood for your next showing."

"But—"

"No buts." Veronica turned her around in place and then gave her a nudge toward the door. "Go."

At least Veronica was right about one thing—not that she knew it—taking photos was the best way to calm Siobhan's frazzled nerves.

Using a small telephoto lens, she'd zoomed in through the front window and taken pictures of her pictures. Even from out here, they looked sensational. For a short second, she felt like such a fraud. Redirecting the lens, she'd snapped photos of Jack carrying crates of wine. Did that man know how to wear a tailored shirt or what?

Through the open doorway, she spotted her brother Chase staring at one of her pictures. She could barely hear what was being said, but she saw Jack come stand behind him and heard his soft voice say, "Your sister is amazing."

Chase's head bobbed. "Yeah, I think I'm starting to get it." Chase turned to Jack and extended his hand. "I'm really sorry about how I behaved."

"No need. Had I been in your shoes I would have reacted the same, maybe worse."

For a second Siobhan forgot about the photos she was taking, about the sandwich board on the sidewalk, her name—Siobhan Baron, Photographer—on the sign, her photos on the walls inside, and the show that would be starting in only another hour or so. All she could think about was how much she loved the two men now laughing inside at who knew what.

Her gaze frozen on the unfolding scene inside, the camera rested on her chest. The weight of it something she'd become accustom to. Like an extension of who she was.

Plenty of people had been walking along the sidewalk, but all had steered clear of her as she'd been snapping away. Except one man who bumped into her, almost knocking her off her feet. Instinctively, her fingers tightened on the camera seconds before the strap pressed hard against the back of her neck.

Her gaze dropped to the camera and the beefy fingers folded around the sides, yanking it away from her. Spinning around and practically slamming into another man in her vain effort to escape Beefy Fingers, her mouth fell open about to yell at the inconsiderate oaf when her gaze landed on the second man's face.

"You sure this is it?"

"I'm not sure of anything. It's a camera and she's using it so this has to be it."

Again her mouth opened, only this time a strong arm pulled her hard against a wall of human flesh as another hand slammed over her mouth. Her muffled moan barely coming through.

"Keep your mouth shut and you won't get hurt."

Through his tight grip, she somehow managed to nod. A whole different kind of panic seized her. This was the face she'd photographed. Who the heck were these guys, and more frighteningly, what did they want with her?

"Rather bold tie for you, isn't it?" Chase tipped his head at Jack as if that would dull the bright colored tie.

"Siobhan talked me into it."

Lips pressed tightly together, Chase nodded as he stared at the tie, then looked up at Jack. "You're really serious about all this, aren't you?"

He bobbed his head and resisted the urge to respond with the old come back *as a heart attack.*

Chase blew out a small sigh and gave a curt nod.

"Okay. Maybe I get it." Then he turned and walked away without another word, leaving Jack staring after his back.

Had anyone asked Jack even an hour ago if he thought the Baron brothers would be coming around to accepting him with Siobhan, he would have thought no way. When he descended on the ranch after the break in, Kyle had actually told Jack to back off and stay away. Only the Governor's intervention that night had convinced Kyle to not break both of Jack's legs. Then there was Mitch. The sensible one, who had the audacity to ask Jack what would it cost to make him go away. That particular little conversation had him so dumfounded, he didn't think the Governor's or Eve's efforts would be enough to bring Mitch back to reality, and yet, somehow, all the brothers had been less volatile the last week. Yes, they'd been surprisingly civil. No sneers, no muttering, no more bribes, but no one seemed truly at ease with the idea of him dating their baby sister. Until now.

"Oh my God!" Paige's voice shouted from the back of the gallery by the temporary bar.

Every head in the room turned, following the direction of her finger. A collective gasp could be heard as each person registered what they were watching. Two men hovered around Siobhan, one tugging at her camera, the other walking away backwards from the gallery with Siobhan clamped tightly in his arms, his hand over her mouth. It took a second, but he'd recognized the man as one of the two men in the park that day. Damn it! He should have been more careful.

Acid churned in Jack's stomach and rose to the back of his mouth as he turned and raced across the gallery, Chase on his heels.

Paige already had her phone open and her voice, several nervous octaves higher than usual, was shouting at the person on the other end, "My sister is being kidnapped!"

Kidnapped. Already out of the line of sight from inside the gallery, Jack's heart nearly stopped at the thought of what those two hoodlums might do to her. He had to get to her in time. Bolting out the door, he could hear footsteps stomping after him.

Sheer panic, mixed with something he couldn't quite put his finger on, danced in Siobhan's eyes.

"Let her go!" he shouted as loud as he could, hoping to startle the men into letting go, or like they'd done in the park, walking away. Only this time, he hoped the police Paige had called arrived in time to catch them.

"All we want is the camera and no one will get hurt," the man with his filthy hands all over Siobhan spat at him.

"Fine. Let her go."

Now Chase stood beside him, his fists clenched at his side.

Jack had to wonder if these men even knew Siobhan was a Baron. If they'd been the same ones to break into the house, they had to. Either way he needed to stop them.

Neither of the two men seemed to notice the red sports car that had pulled up and parked a few feet away from them. Jack had never been happier to see Kyle in his entire life. Now if only Kyle figured out what was happening before the men realized they were outnumbered.

"What the hell?" Kyle stormed up, creating a scene. So much for the element of surprise.

The guy who now held Siobhan's camera spun around and swung at Kyle. He clearly hadn't expected to literally run into a man who was a professional athlete in excellent shape with reflexes to match. Swinging and missing a second time, the guy almost toppled over.

That wild look of a trapped animal blossomed in the eyes of the man still hanging onto Siobhan for dear life.

Chase doubled around Jack, and jumped into the fray in an effort to help Kyle subdue the guy still hanging onto Siobhan's camera. They looked like a couple of young monkeys hanging onto their mother's backs. This was not good.

"Let her go." Jack waved at the two still backing away. Now he could see Eve had circled around, probably from the back of the gallery, and held a wine bottle in her hand. What the hell was she going to do… offer him a drink?

"Not on your life. We want those photos. Now."

"You can have whatever you want if you'll let the lady

go." He dared to inch a little closer.

To Jack's right, Paige was off the phone and easing her way closer to him. From the way she kept one hand on her purse, he knew that could only mean one thing—she was carrying. He blew out a slow deep breath. Just what he needed, stray bullets flying and Siobhan in the middle of it.

So focused on Siobhan and the crazy man still dragging her away, Jack hadn't noticed where Craig had come from, but the three brothers had the idiot with the camera on the ground, his hands behind his back, manacled with someone's tie, and Kyle practically sitting on the guy.

When he noticed from the corner of his eye that Paige had barely nodded at her younger sister, he wanted to shout at Paige not to draw and to let him handle it, but there'd been no time. All of a sudden, he saw both Siobhan and Eve barely nod and blink back at her. In seconds, Siobhan lifted her knee, and a three-inch spike heel, something very uncharacteristic for his girl, came crashing down on the idiot's arch. As she'd probably hoped, the shock of it, or the pain, had him releasing his hold on her. At the same moment, Eve brought the bottle of wine crashing down on his head.

The guy from the photo fell to the ground, writhing in pain, unsure of what aching body part to grab onto.

"Want me to kick him for you?" Eve asked her little sister.

Glaring at the man on the floor, Siobhan shook her head. "Nah, you'd probably break him."

"You little bi—" Rubbing the back of his head, the man stopped speaking mid sentence.

Jack spotted the same thing the guy had, Paige stood over him, her 9 mm short barrel handgun pointed directly at the stupid man.

"Temper, temper." Paige's words dripped with sarcasm. "What would your mother say if she could hear you now?"

With the sound of sirens growing closer, all the man could do was groan and give up the fight.

All Jack could do was hurry to Siobhan's side. "You okay?"

Nodding at him, she practically fell into his arms. "I think I'm fine."

"Thank God." He pulled her tighter against him, and lowering his head, whispered, "I love you, Siobhan Baron, and I do not—ever—want to lose you."

Her head pulled away from him, and her chin lifted up until their gazes met. "Ditto."

Siobhan had never been so scared in her entire life. Risk was a common denominator in the Baron family. She'd raced sailboats, driven fast cars, and even swam with sharks, but this guy's hands wrapped around her was a whole different level of fear. As relieved as she was to see Jack racing out of the gallery to come to her aid, not till she spotted both Eve and Paige did she realize, they could do this.

"Do you remember seeing this man before?" the officer asked, dragging her out of her own thoughts.

"I think he's the same guy from the park." She'd already told the other officer the same thing. She didn't mind answering questions, she just wished they weren't all the same ones.

His thumb drawing calming swirls on her hand, Jack paused. "I recognized the other guy. They were both from the park that day."

Scribbling in a little notebook, the officer nodded before glancing up at them. "The guy your brothers tackled, accidentally admitted that they're the ones who broke into your house looking for the camera."

"Why do they want my camera?" she asked softly.

"Don't know." The officer shrugged. "He realized what he'd said and lawyered up before we could get any more answers, but we'll get to the bottom of this."

"Thank you, officer." Jack extended his hand to the policeman. "Please keep us updated."

The cop nodded.

"Do you think there's any more danger?" Siobhan hated asking the question, but she wasn't going to feel safe again until she knew everyone involved was safely and permanently locked behind bars.

"I can't say at this time, but I suggest you remain vigilant and close to family. The detective assigned to this will let you know what's happening."

"Thank you." She hoped she'd have answers sooner than later.

The policeman stepped aside and Jack turned to face her. "You doing okay?"

"Much to my surprise, yes."

The first smile she'd seen all day bloomed. "You wield a mean spiked heel."

That made her smile. "I do, don't I?"

"You're amazing." He squeezed her hand.

"Back at you." Right now, she didn't care who was watching, she grabbed onto the brassy tie she'd talked him into buying and pulled him in closer. "You, Jack Preston, are my hero."

CHAPTER SEVENTEEN

"This is silly."

Jack had spent the better part of the last week putting together this surprise for Siobhan. The last thing he wanted was for her to guess before he was ready. "I was afraid if I wrapped a bandana or something across your eyes, folks driving by would think I'd kidnapped you."

"Well, you did. Sort of." She giggled. "But don't you think those same drivers will be a little suspicious seeing me wearing a sleep mask?"

He shook his head before he remembered she couldn't see him. "No. They'll probably think you want a nap and don't want the sun in your face."

"Maybe, but don't be surprised if flashing lights come flying up behind you any time now."

That was the last thing he needed. They were already running a bit behind schedule.

"How much longer before I can take this thing off and open my eyes?"

Jack chuckled. "Be patient."

"For the record, patience is overrated." Before she could present further argument, her cell phone sounded and crossing her arms, she shifted to face him even though she couldn't see him. "Do I get to answer my phone?"

Extending his arm, he uncurled his fingers. "Hand it to me."

This time she huffed before pulling the phone out of her pocket and giving it to him. He tapped answer and speaker phone. "Hello."

"Hey, Siobhan." Veronica's tone was more upbeat than

usual. "Guess what I just sold?"

The corners of Siobhan's mouth shifted from a slight pout to an easy smile. "Urban or nature shots?"

"Actually, both."

"Both?" The way her forehead creased, he didn't have to see her eyes to know they had to have popped open wide.

"We just sold the entire central display. The buyer wanted the urban collection for one wall of his study and a handful of your national parks photos for his actual office. Are you sitting down?"

Siobhan nodded. "Yes."

"Sweetie, the total sales amount came to forty-five thousand."

Without saying a word, her hand landed palm open on her chest. "Forty…"

"…five thousand," Veronica finished for her. "Five thousand each for the smaller prints and ten for the one with the little girl laughing."

"Wow, just wow."

Veronica laughed heartily. "You'd better find something else to shoot. I told them they can't pick the photos up until the exhibit is over, and the man was less than thrilled but had no choice."

That little tidbit of information subdued the unease that had crept in when Veronica mentioned the sale. The last thing Jack needed was for the collection to dwindle before he got everyone back to the gallery this afternoon.

"I can't believe it." Siobhan took in a calming breath.

"I don't do shows as favors. I don't care who my friends are or who your grandfather is, I told you that you had a great eye. I hope you'll continue to let me show your best pieces as they come in."

"Absolutely."

"Hate to interrupt, but we're here." Jack pulled into a space and cut the engine.

"Have to run, Veronica. Thanks so much for calling."

While she said her goodbyes and hung up, Jack ran around to open the car door.

"Now can I take this silly eye mask off?"

As much as he'd rather she kept it on till the last minute so she'd have less time to figure out his surprise, he doubted that would go over well with the observing public. "Yes."

Whipping the thing off with more gusto than he would have expected, she stared up at the building in front of them. "The airport?"

"Just a quick stop." He grabbed hold of her hand and squeezed.

"The airport? You kept me in the dark—literally—for the airport?"

He squeezed her hand. "Trust me."

Leveling her gaze with his, the look in her eyes softened. "You know I do."

And knowing the truth of her words made his heart hammer even harder in his chest. So many moving parts had to happen for this little surprise to work. He'd considered buying tickets for anywhere to get them into security, but then he decided that there were too many ways that choice could backfire, so instead, he'd made sure they arrived late enough that they wouldn't be standing at the baggage claim waiting.

"The airport," she muttered again as they crossed the pavement between building and parking lot.

The second they walked through the doors, heads turned, they always did when Siobhan was at his side. Last night they'd been to a party at the country club. The moment they'd crossed the threshold all the guys in the place focused on Siobhan. He knew exactly what they were thinking. Every one of them probably wished she were there with them, but she wasn't. She was with him. As every eye followed her, in his heart he kept thinking, *nope*, she's *my* girl.

Working from a photograph he'd found online, it didn't take him long to recognize who they'd come to meet at the airport. It took Siobhan a fraction longer to connect the dots. When the woman turned fully to face them and flashed a bright smile, Siobhan flew into open arms and squealed, "Mum!"

Siobhan couldn't believe her eyes. "I thought you couldn't get away from work?"

"That's what I thought." Maura Baron shrugged. "But apparently, someone," her gaze shot over Siobhan's shoulder to where Jack stood quietly watching, "convinced my boss that Samantha could fill in for me for a few weeks and the business wouldn't crumble."

"Well, I'm very glad of that." Looking over her shoulder, she blew Jack a silent kiss.

"And you," her mother sidestepped her daughter and walked up to Jack, "are my miracle worker."

One shoulder hefted up in a casual shrug. "It wasn't that hard."

Her mum shook her head. "I know full well all the strings you had to pull to get that old goat to let someone else handle the viscount's wedding reception."

"I may have mentioned something about securing a prominent wedding or two for his venue in the near future."

"Prominent?" Her mum laughed and looked at Siobhan. "He actually got a prince to call my boss and book the venue for his wedding next year. Not his admin, or secretary, but the prince himself."

Siobhan looked from Jack to her mother. "Which prince?"

"I don't know, or care, one of those nine hundred little principalities scattered around Europe, but Mr. Borner was over the moon and more than happy to let me come see your show."

Was there no end to how sweet Jack could be? Siobhan wanted so badly to kiss his socks off, but this was neither the time nor the place.

"Which are your bags?" Jack asked.

Her mother pointed to two large wheeled suitcases at her side. "I can hardly wait to see the show in person. I knew it would be a smashing success. And I bet it has all been so much fun too."

"It's been an amazing ride." She still didn't believe all this was happening so fast.

Jack sighed. "I could have done without the idiots trying to steal you and your camera."

"Wait." Her mum came to a stop. "What do you mean steal you?"

"Well. The key word is *try*." Siobhan hadn't seen the need to tell her mother about the two guys from the park, and until now hadn't seen a need to tell Jack that she hadn't shared that little tidbit about the exhibit's opening day. "I didn't realize at the time, but the park not far from Jack's place has a bit of a seedy reputation."

Her mother's brows rose a little higher but she wasn't moving.

"Maybe," Jack gestured toward the doors, "we should explain this in the car."

Without a word, her mother nodded and began walking. "Start explaining now."

His hands full with her mother's bags, Jack gave her an encouraging nod.

"As I mentioned, unbeknownst to me, the park is known to the locals for being a gang hangout and a base for drug deals."

"Oh, no." Her mum gasped.

"Yeah. Apparently, I not only photographed a drug deal going down without realizing it, I also got a photo of one of the ringleaders, if that's what they're called. Needless to say, they wanted my camera back badly."

"Does this have something to do with the break in at the ranch?" her mother asked.

Siobhan nodded. "Yep. Turns out they'd been following me for days. They'd first spooked me the day I took the photos. They had stayed close to me—"

"Too close," Jack interrupted.

"Agreed. Too close to me in hopes of simply grabbing the camera without me noticing, but then Jack showed up and they abandoned that idea. Instead, they struck the ranch house once it was empty, but didn't know that my cameras were not in my room but my workshop. The fact that we're

Barons wasn't enough to scare them off."

"But," Jack interjected, "everyone is now safely behind bars awaiting trial."

"Is bail a risk?"

Jack shook his head. "Let's just say there are a few good reasons not to go up against the Baron family."

"Good." Her mother looped an arm around her waist. "Hopefully, you'll be old and gray before they get out of jail."

"That's the plan." Jack smiled at them, then opening the hatch of his SUV with the fob, tossed the two suitcases into the back as if they were nothing more than a pair of pillows. "Next stop the gallery."

In the car, settled and buckled in, Siobhan thought about what her mother had said about Jack pulling strings. "Exactly how did you get a prince involved in getting Mum here?"

Backing out of the parking space, Jack shrugged. "I met a lot of important people hanging out with your brother on the racing circuit. As it so happened, I also made this particular prince a great deal of money. Calling in a favor wasn't very difficult. Your mother's stellar reputation made it even easier to convince the bride and groom that there was no better place for a royal reception."

This man was seriously thoughtful and down right amazing. Reaching over the console, she squeezed Jack's hand and mouthed, 'I love you.'

With a wide smile on his face, he mouthed back, 'love you more.' Siobhan's heart did a now familiar two-step. Could life get any sweeter than this?

EPILOGUE

If there was one thing Lila Baron loved, it was a party. Mitch's grandmother could write the book on being the perfect hostess. Whether it was a comic-themed birthday bash, a nineteen fifties sock hop graduation party, or a Gatsby-themed engagement soiree, Lila Baron would guarantee a party the guests would never forget. Siobhan's engagement party was exactly that.

"You look very pensive." His sister Paige handed him a glass of wine. "Care to share?"

"I'm afraid there's nothing salacious involved. Just thinking how Grams loves a good party and how pretty much everyone in Houston covets an invitation to one of her events." And when his grandmother put on a party, it was always the event of the year.

"Oh, that she does." Paige took a sip from her wine glass. "I can't believe she talked Siobhan into this big shindig."

"The kid seems so happy, I think Grams could have talked her into an engagement party in a cave with nothing but vampire bats in attendance."

"We've been over this, she's not a kid. Not anymore."

Deep down he knew that, but he suspected even when she starts collecting social security, he'd still be calling her kid. Though it took a while for him to stop growling at Jack. Once he finally saw past the fury and took a look—a good look—he saw what his grandmother and sisters had been telling him. That same head over heels look that had been in his brothers' eyes at finding the right woman, was shining brightly for all to see in Jack's eyes. And Siobhan's too.

Even now. They were halfway across the outdoor tent

and the electricity between them was so strong Mitch was pretty sure if anyone bumped into them, they'd get burned.

"They do look wonderful, don't they?" Paige took another sip of wine. "Reminds me a little of you and Abbie."

Is that what he and his late wife looked like? If Jack Preston loved Siobhan even half as much as he had loved Abbie, then they'd be the luckiest two people in the world.

"Except he's a better dancer than you are." Paige bumped him with her hip.

That snapped him out of his melancholy and brought a smile to his face and the deep-rooted sense of competition that ran through every Baron's veins soared. "I'll have you know I'm an excellent dancer." To prove his point, he grabbed his sister by the hand and spun her into a dance pose without spilling a drop of the wine in her glass.

"Okay," Paige chuckled, "maybe you are better."

Paige turned her attention back to the newly engaged couple.

"Did I really look at Abbie that way?"

His sister nodded. "You did. I remember the first time you brought her to the ranch for Sunday supper. Every time she opened her mouth, you looked at her as if she was about to spew forth holy scripture. I knew then she was the one and only for you."

And wasn't that the problem? He truly believed in the love of a lifetime, but he'd already had his. There'd be no second chances for him.

"All of you look at the women you love that way. I'd like to think Daniel looks at me like that."

"He does." Mitch had noticed the connection between Paige and Daniel early on. If he hadn't been so angry at the idea of Jack taking advantage of his youngest sister, he probably would have seen the love there sooner.

"Oh, man." Paige waved a finger at her sister. "I didn't think people dipped anymore. Look at them. They haven't taken their eyes off each other, and more importantly, he didn't drop her."

"He wouldn't dare."

Paige chuckled again. The music had stopped and the couple of honor had shifted from the dance floor to making the rounds, thanking the guests for coming. Their grandmother had trained them all well. Even as the happy couple maneuvered through the crowd, they continued to hold hands, and every so often would stop to stare up at each other. If he didn't know better, Mitch would swear those two were about to self combust. Something told him this wedding was going to happen sooner rather than later.

When they reached the table where Jack's mother and father were seated, he leaned over to give his mother a huge hug. Arms open wide, Mrs. Preston gave Siobhan an equally big hug. While the two women chatted contentedly, Jack wandered away and returned with fresh drinks for his parents. The conversation between mother and future daughter-in-law continued while Jack walked away again, returning with a dish overflowing with desserts, and set it in front of his mother. The woman beamed at him, and Jack's smile bloomed as he leaned over to kiss his mother on the cheek again.

"You know," Paige took a quick sip of her drink, "they say you can tell how a man will treat his wife by the way he treats his mother. I'd say Siobhan has it made in the shade."

Mitch simply nodded. He really shouldn't have given Jack such a hard time. If his kid sister ever found out that Mitch actually tried to pay Jack off to leave her alone, she'd probably hang him from the nearest tree by his toes.

"Here they come." Paige elbowed her brother. "Don't want them to know we've been staring."

"They have to know everyone has been watching them. They are the guests of honor, after all."

Still holding hands, Jack and Siobhan joined them at the family table.

"I never realized how much work is involved in being the reason for the party." Somehow, Jack managed to pull the chair out for his bride-to-be without letting go of her hand.

Siobhan smiled up at her fiancé. "Maybe we should elope and avoid the whole thing. I mean, this little bash is big enough of a party, not sure I have it in me to do this all over again."

As far as Mitch knew, every woman under the sun dreamed of a big Cinderella wedding. Not his baby sister.

"I think Grams would have a heart attack." Paige shrugged. "She lives for weddings."

"I know." Siobhan sighed and Jack seamlessly let go of her hand and draped his arm across her shoulders, delicately caressing her with his thumb, quickly drawing another smile from her.

Once again, he had to ask himself, how had he and his brothers missed how perfect these two were for each other? And to think he and the other Baron brothers could have kept their heads up their butts and ruined all this for Siobhan. Once upon a time he'd been a great judge of character. Lately, he seemed incapable of properly reading situations. What had happened to him?

"You still with us?" Paige cleared her throat.

"Sorry. Mind wandered."

"Mm." His sister's mouth twisted to one side. "Is it Abbie?"

He shook his head. With every passing day, the memory of Abbie's smile faded just a little bit more. "Just thinking how glad I am that we didn't mess this up for the lovebirds."

"I'm just glad Chase stopped punching the poor guy in the face."

Mitch chuckled. "At least Jack doesn't have a glass jaw."

"Thankfully," Paige agreed with a smile.

When Jack and Siobhan thought the rest of the table was too engrossed in conversation to notice, the two stole a kiss. Mitch could feel the heat in the quick peck clear across the table. Oh, how he missed that magic, but he'd had his chance at happily ever after. Now it was Siobhan's turn, and if there was one thing he was convinced of, whether they eloped or had a blowout party, this marriage would last forever.

★

Enjoy an excerpt from
Just One Chance

"There you go." Mitchell Baron blew out a long deep breath and for the first time in hours, a smile graced his features.

Claire stretched her back, leaning left then right. "It's never fun when the first thing you see is only one hoof."

"That's probably what Mama was thinking." Watching the healthy calf latch onto its mother was the perfect end to a long night.

"I bet she was happy to have you with her." The oldest girl in Uncle Everett's clan, Claire was only eleven months younger than her brother Devlin, and thankfully for the Paradise Ridge Ranch, one helluva veterinarian. "Glad you called me in. Hate it when I get the call after the mom has suffered for way too long. Hate it even more when we lose mom and or the calf because I didn't get a call at all."

"When she passed three hours of labor I knew something was off. Her last calf came in just over two. The way she kept looking at me, I just knew."

"That is a gift I wish more of my ranchers had. Turning the calf is not easy, but it's better than letting nature take its course and losing her. You did good calling me before the calf presented."

"I suppose it helps knowing you're family and won't tell me to go to hell for waking you up at three o'clock in the morning with a hunch."

She chuckled before her expression turned serious. "I don't even want to ask what you were doing awake all night in the barn. That's not your job." Always too smart for her own good, Claire raised a single brow at him before shaking her head and stretching her back one more time. "On the bright side, being up at this hour means that I'll be rewarded with Hazel's breakfast."

"Thank heaven for Hazel." His hand on the small of his cousin's back, Mitch led Claire toward the house. The barn had always been a place of refuge for him. As a kid when his brothers, whom he loved dearly, were in over-the-top rowdy mode, later when the stress of exams threatened to crush him, or when the senior politicians' stubbornness drove him crazy…to when he lost Abbie.

More than three years had gone by since his wife died, and yet, the ache was still so strong and real that some days it almost stole his breath away. But that wasn't what had kept him running home from Washington more and more. Tonight it was another text from Susan that had him seeking solace with the animals in the barn.

The moment he and his cousin crossed the threshold into the heart of the family ranch, the smell of fresh baked cinnamon rolls mixed with a hint of bacon frying, assaulted his senses. He had no idea why bacon smelled so much better when Hazel made it, but it did.

"Thought y'all would be hungry." Spatula in hand, Hazel turned to smile at the two of them. "Table's set in the dining room. Coffee is hot. Your grandfather has already eaten and is off to some committee meeting. Y'all are on your own until the rest of the family wakes."

Claire snatched a piece of bacon from a plate on the counter, and Hazel smacked her hand. "None of that till the eggs are done. Off to the dining room."

Crunching on the stolen morsel, Claire giggled like a schoolgirl.

He loved that laugh. She sounded just like his sister Eve. Her laugh would make him smile as well. It was Eve who more than anyone in the family had helped keep him somewhat together when Abbie died.

His phone beeped and he pulled it from his pocket and swiped at it, quickly putting it back. A few seconds later it beeped again. Once more, he pulled it out and swiped at it.

"Aren't you even going to see who it's from?"

"I know who it's from."

Claire's eyebrows rose up and down on her forehead a few times. "A woman?"

"Yes." He let out a slow sigh. "But not the way you're thinking."

"Oh, okay." It was clear from her tone she didn't believe him.

"Susan is only a colleague."

"Susan?" Now Claire was smiling at him.

He had no idea how she could chew and grin at the same time. "We're on the same committee. She and I were the only two on the same side."

"Were?"

"Are. We are on the same side, but sometimes fighting the political wheel makes swimming upstream in a river of sharks feel like an easy and safe endeavor."

"Oh, doesn't that sound like fun. I guess it helps having an ally."

Ally. That was one word for Susan. "It did."

"Did?"

"I think Washington politics is wearing thin on me."

The humor in Claire's eyes dimmed. "Sorry. I know how much you used to love it."

"That's what I keep telling myself."

His phone beeped again and this time he looked at it.

THOUGHT YOU WERE STAYING TILL THE END OF SESSION. ARE YOU COMING BACK FOR THE VOTE?

Quickly running his fingers over the keyboard, he typed a simple answer. *YES.* Of course he was going back. Didn't he always? He might spend every weekend he could in Texas, but he had never missed a meeting, a debate, or a vote before, and he wasn't going to start now. No matter what, or who, chased him away.

Gwyneth Van Klein focused carefully on the small wooden box in her hands. On her twenty-first birthday, she'd taken refuge in her father's library from the boring family gathering her mother had orchestrated. The supposed party intended to celebrate her crossing into legal adulthood. The idea was almost funny, as if her mother would ever let her be an adult. Deep down, she'd understood that even then.

Having noticed a book off kilter with the others on the shelf, something her mother would never have stood for, Gwyneth pulled the offending book out of the line. Hidden behind the row of tomes, she'd uncovered her father's little stash. Tools and materials for fine carving. They were hidden inside a box he'd no doubt etched himself. A beautiful piece of art. She would never have expected something so whimsical from the head of Klein Electronics. The discovery had the corners of her mouth tilting up in her first smile of the day. Knowing that her mother would never approve of such a mundane and common hobby actually made her a little happy. The idea that someone in the family had the nerve to stand up, even in hiding, to her mother had been her best birthday gift.

When she'd discreetly informed her father of her discovery the next day, she'd been eager for him to show her how to use the tools. For the first time in her life, she'd had something to look forward to that her mother couldn't somehow remove from her world, or worse, destroy. The unexpected reward had been finding a connection with one of her parents. For the next few months, as her father shared with her how to gently maneuver the sharp-tipped tool to create what she hoped would some day be beautiful works of craftsmanship, she'd actually enjoyed herself, and her father's company. But even more surprising, she truly felt that her father enjoyed passing his beloved hobby onto her. Not her brothers, her.

That brief time of true contentment in her life came to a crashing end when alone in his office, her father suffered a massive coronary. By the time his secretary grew curious about the lack of communication from her boss, it had been too late to save him.

That had been over a decade ago and the only contentment in her life remained the pride at finishing another work. Nora, one of the housekeeping staff, had been her comrade in arms. Nora would help her purchase the supplies without her mother's knowledge, and then arrange for the sale of the completed project in a local artist's gallery. The little money she received was just enough to keep her busy. And sane.

Setting down the sharp tool, she reached into her dressing table drawer. Sneaking a snack from her sacred stash of cookies and treats. Another thing for which she counted on Nora. After all, snack foods loaded with sugars and artificial preservatives served, according to Prudence Van Klein, only one purpose: to destroy the refined appearance and slim figure of weak-willed and indulgent females. Not that anyone would notice anything about Gwyneth's figure under the frumpy wardrobe her mother sparingly purchased for her. The only things missing from the mid-century schoolmarm look were the laced up sensible shoes. Though in some ways, her sensible pumps weren't a far cry from the shoes she remembered her grandmother wearing.

"Miss," her name sounded, followed by a light rap on her door. It was Nora. "Your mother is expecting you downstairs. Right away. She seems rather eager."

The mere mention of being summoned by her mother for something 'eager' had her hand slipping. The tiny notch would be almost imperceptible to the average person, but not to her. As with so many other things in her life, she tossed the scarred carving into the trash. "Tell Mother I shall be down momentarily."

Standing a moment in front of the mirror, not because she had anything to admire, but because every hair and stitch needed to be perfectly in place before she descended the stairs, she reluctantly surveyed her appearance. Her sleeves were past her elbow, a true accomplishment to have convinced her mother that long sleeves were unnecessary in the miserable Texas heat. The hem of her dress, not a skirt, and not slacks, a dress, was exactly six inches below the knee and perfectly straight. Of course, she wore hose even though no one else her age, and in their right mind, would do so on sweltering days. Early in her childhood her naturally curly hair had been deemed an unruly mess by her mother. Always tamed into braids longer than appropriate for any child, now every strand of hair was neatly plastered along her scalp and twisted into a perfectly rounded bun at the back of her head. All would meet with her mother's approval. Just not a man's. At least not one in his right mind.

"There you are." As she reached the doorway, her mother looked up from her game of solitaire. The old-fashioned way, of course, with a deck of cards. "I sent Nora for you almost five minutes ago."

"Yes, Mother. I'm sorry to have kept you waiting."

"Never mind." Still looking at the cards in front of her, the older woman waved at Gwyneth to sit. "I have wonderful news."

Somehow, she felt the need to brace herself.

"The Barons are hosting the Cattleman's pre-ball gala at their home this year."

Gwyneth nodded. The Barons were as far up the social register as the Van Kleins, though it was the Conroe pedigree that her mother admired, not so much the common bloodline the Governor had brought to the genetic pool.

"The guest list is, of course, limited to the right people."

Which meant her brothers would be on the list. Klein Electronics was only one of many corporations that continued to fill the family coffers and guarantee invitations to the most exclusive parties.

Her mother looked up from her cards. "The gala will be three weeks from Friday next."

Gwyneth refrained from groaning. Anyone would think her mother had fallen off a time travel machine. Who in today's world said Friday next?

"Your brothers have previous commitments and cannot escort me." Her mother returned to turning cards. "I've decided you and I shall accept the invitation."

Accept? Her and her mother? Gwyneth's palms began to sweat. Dread squeezed her lungs. She didn't do well at large parties. Or small ones. People always stared at her, or more so the way her mother would make her dress. Then all the whispers would start, usually starting with *poor Gwyneth*. She hated every minute of it. She didn't want people's polite smiles with pity filled eyes. She wanted to stay in her room and work on her art until she grew too old to know that life had passed her by.

"In the meantime," her mother continued, once again looking down at her cards, "Mrs. Baron is having an afternoon tea this coming Saturday. We shall be attending."

A gala and a tea? What had come over her mother? And why was Prudence Van Klein dragging her awkward and ill-fitting daughter along with her? Something was definitely up, and heaven help her, whatever it was, Gwyneth was sure of one thing, none of it could possibly end well for her.

Read more of Just One Chance available now

MEET CHRIS

Author of over fifty contemporary novels, including the award winning Aloha Series, Chris Keniston lives in North Texas with her husband, two adult children, and two canine children. Though she loves her puppies equally, she admits being especially attached to her German Shepherd rescue. After all, even dogs deserve a happily ever after.

More on Chris and her books can be found at www.chris keniston.com.

Follow Chris on facebook at ChrisKenistonAuthor or on twitter @ckenistonauthor.

Join Chris' newsletter! Enjoy inside peeks from Chris' world and stories, receive notification of new releases, and sometimes she'll thank her subscribers with a free copy of a new 99 cent flirt.

Please, if you enjoyed reading Just One Shot, consider helping other readers find the Billionaire Barons of Texas Series by taking a moment to leave a review. Reviews are a blessing to authors and readers alike. Even just a few words will do! Thank you.